ACTING NAUGHTY

ACTING NAUGHTY
Book One of the Action! Series
Copyright © G.A. HAUSER, 2008
Cover art by Beverly Maxwell
ISBN Trade paperback: 978-1-60202-161-7
ISBN MS Reader (LIT): 978-1-60202-160-0

Linden Bay Romance, LLC
577 Mulberry Street, Suite 1520
Macon, GA 31201
www.lindenbayromance.com

First Linden Bay Romance publication: January 2009

ACTING NAUGHTY

Book One in the Action! Series

BY G.A. HAUSER

Prologue

"Adam, Keith O'Leary is on line one."

"Thanks, Natalie." Adam Lewis sat down at his desk and picked up the phone. "Keith?"

"Hey, Adam."

"Have you read the script?"

"I have."

Adam detected some hesitation in his voice. "Look, Keith, I know it's not what you were initially after. But before you turn it down, let me tell you how many other roles I've tried to hook you up with without success. Don't reject it outright until you've thought long and hard about it."

"Adam…I understand that and I do appreciate it."

"But?" He tried not to grow angry.

"I have to touch another guy."

"I know. Forget it, all right?" Adam rubbed his forehead, hating the fact that he had been sending out Keith's headshots and credentials for three months and no one was offering him a thing.

"Don't get angry with me, Adam."

"I am. Let me tell you why, Keith." Sitting up in his chair, he forced himself to speak calmly. "Forever Young is the hottest new drama on cable television at the moment. Okay? People would kill to get an audition, let alone an offer for a steady paycheck. Once you are in as a main character, you're set for years. Are you listening to me?"

"Yes."

"I haven't been totally honest with you because before this offer I didn't want to crush you, but I have to tell you, Keith, because of your…" Adam wanted to say it gently, but decided to just be blunt, "…your pretty looks. No one wants you."

Keith groaned. "Pretty?"

"Yes. I'm sorry to be the bearer of bad news, Keith." Adam

laughed at the irony of the conversation. "But, you're fucking pretty. Okay?"

"What should I do? Shave my head and grow a beard?"

"Oh, hell no. You'd never get work at all." Adam straightened his back and stared down at the paperwork on his desk. "Please, don't reject it based solely because you have to have contact with another male actor. And that's why they call it acting, Keith. Remember?"

"I just don't know if I can do it."

"Fine. I'll tell them you've declined the offer. Just don't whine when nothing comes in for you for another six months. It's not because I'm not trying."

"Hang on. Don't call them just yet."

Exhaling in annoyance, Adam had too many other phone calls to make to get bogged down with this kind of indecision. "I have to call them, Keith. If I don't, they'll offer it to someone else."

"Go over the figures again. How much?"

Wishing he had sent a gay man to do the job, Adam cupped the phone to shout, "Natalie!"

"Yes, boss?"

"Can you find the offer for Keith O'Leary for the role of Dennis Jason in Forever Young?"

"Yes. One sec."

He listened to the other end of the phone line. "You still there?"

"I am. I want to discuss it with my girlfriend a little. I mean, this may weird her out as well."

"Why? Jesus, Keith, you're not expected to screw the guy. You know these dramas, if two men kiss it's monumental late night news."

Natalie rushed in with a folder.

"Thanks, Nat." Adam took it and pulled the paperwork out of the envelope. "Right. Ready?"

"Shoot."

Adam read the terms of the contract, including the salary. Once he had he pushed the papers aside, he reclined in his leather chair. "I need to call them sometime today."

"I'll get back to you in an hour."

"Thank you, Keith."

"No, thank you, Adam."

Adam hung up and grumbled, "You better take it, baby, there ain't much out there for you."

Natalie stood at his office door. "Is he passing it up?"

Slipping the paperwork into its folder, he replied, "He's afraid to kiss a man. Believe it?"

Smiling wryly, Natalie approached him to retrieve the folder. "You should invite him over for dinner with you and Jack. Oh, and Steve and Mark."

Adam gave her an impish grin. "That would either convert him or scare the nuts off him."

Natalie left his office, giggling as she went, to sit back at her desk.

Adam kept his smile as he looked at a photo of he and Jack propped up on his desk.

"What did he say, Keith?"

Dropping down on the sofa beside Patty with the pad he had scribbled figures on, Keith showed her the numbers.

"That much?"

"Yes."

"Do it!"

Keith rubbed his face with both hands, leaning over his lap as he considered his options.

Patty curled around him to support him. "Keith, I'm struggling to pay my half of the rent waitressing and you're living off your savings. It's not good."

"I know."

"We both have been dying to get into acting. That soap is awesome. It's the hottest show on cable at the moment."

"I know," he echoed, moaning.

"You'd be insane not to take it! Look!" She held the pad with the amount of his salary on it as if he hadn't been the one to write it.

Flopping back to slouch on the couch, Keith connected to Patty's worried eyes. "Fine. I'll take it."

She wrapped around his neck and kissed his cheek. "Hollywood here you come!"

Adam arrived home seeing Jack's Jaguar parked out front.

Taking off his tie as he entered the house, hearing loud rock music, he peered into their home gym to find his blond hunk pumping iron. "Hello, handsome!"

"Hey, cutie."

"I'll be there as soon as I change."

"Can't wait," Jack replied, pressing an enormous amount of weight over his head while he lay back on a bench.

Ascending the stairs to their bedroom, Adam quickly shed his suit and dressed in a pair of gym shorts and a running top. Carrying his sneakers, he jogged back to the gym and sat down on a bench to tie his laces.

"How was work?" Jack shouted over the loud music.

"Good. Remind me to tell you something."

"Oh?"

"Yes." Adam gave Jack a smile.

After Jack set the weights down on their mounts, he sat up, crossed the room to lower the music. "Now what?"

"No. Nothing like what you're thinking. I know how your mind works, Larsen. I'm not in trouble."

"Good." Jack approached. "Don't I get a kiss hello?"

"Oh. I've been remiss! Get over here, stud." Adam jumped off the bench and onto Jack, wrapping his legs around his hips. Moaning softly at the taste of Jack's mouth, Adam enjoyed a good wet tongue kiss before he paused to stare into Jack's aquamarine eyes. "If we keep this up, we'll screw instead of working out."

Jack set him back on his feet gently. "What happened at work?"

As Adam stood on the treadmill, feeding it his info, he replied, "You know that incredible new cable television series, Forever Young?"

"I do." Jack began adding more weights to his already loaded bar.

"I sent a young, pretty, blue-eyed blond there for an audition for a new character. They loved him. Instantly made an offer."

"And?" Jack lay back down on the bench, adjusting his leather fingerless gloves.

"The guy is twenty-six and hasn't done anything but a few crappy commercials. But...he's damn gorgeous."

"And?" Jack asked with more emphasis.

"He's straight and the role is for him to play a gay partner to one of the regulars."

"Which regular?"

"If I tell you, it'll be a spoiler."

"Adam…" Jack chided.

"For Troy Wright. The character that plays the son of Sylvia and Marty. The actor's name is Carl Bronson."

"He's going to be gay?" Jack laughed. "I love that show."

"I know. He's fricken hot. Do you believe this client, Keith, almost turned it down because he has to touch the guy?"

"I'd touch him."

"Hey! You will not."

"I'm teasing. So? Is he taking the part?"

"He is. He called me right before I left the office." Adam began a slow jog to warm up. "Jack, he'd be nuts not to. The money is phenomenal, and if his character melds well with the existing cast, he could have a job for years."

"He wouldn't be the first straight man to play a gay role. What's the big deal? Gay guys play straight roles all the time."

"Shh, that's a secret." Adam winked.

Chapter One

Keith showed his pass to the guard at the studio gate. He was allowed in and parked in a shady spot in the lot. Sitting for a moment to study his directions for the correct building, he climbed out and chirped the lock on his Subaru.

Getting lost, Keith asked someone rushing by, "Excuse me, can you help me out?"

The person pointed him in the right direction and he hurried to the correct door. Once again showing his pass, he gained entry. As he wandered to where all the voices were coming from he instantly recognized the set designs for Forever Young, along with the well known cast. His pulse raced in excitement. This had to be good for his career.

"Yes, hello, I'm Keith O'Leary. I'm here for my first day—"

"Go meet the director."

The man hurried passed Keith quickly. Swallowing his nerves, Keith found a petite woman standing in a crowd of the main characters of the drama slash soap. Behind her a chair with the word "director" painted on it in white stencil sat vacant.

Moving closer, hearing her giving her opinions, Keith assumed this was the new powerhouse of television drama, Charlotte Deavers.

Someone spotted him and tapped Charlotte on the shoulder, gesturing to him. When she spun around, Keith gulped a dry lump in his throat.

"Keith!" She rushed towards him with her hand out. "I am so glad to see you. Oh, you are too fantastic! Everyone, this is Keith O'Leary. Hang on, hang on..." she began shouting, "Carl! Where's Carl?"

His hand still clasped in hers, Keith looked to where she was gesturing.

A tall, strikingly handsome man, wearing a pair of faded blue jeans and a sleeveless black T-shirt, holding a script in his hand, turned her way. Keith instantly recognized him as the actor, Carl Bronson. Wow. He may never have touched a guy before but he sure as shit could tell an exceptional one when he spotted one.

"Carl, come here. I want you to meet your new co-star." Charlotte released Keith's hand and stood back, as if she wanted to witness this first contact and absorb it.

Keith's skin broke out in chills. Yes, Carl looked good on television, but Keith had no idea how tall, nor how incredibly muscular he was without all the heavy clothing he wore in the show. Keith felt small by comparison, being only five foot eleven.

"Carl, this is Keith O'Leary. He's playing your new squeeze, Dennis Jason."

"Nice to meet you."

Keith reached out for his hand. It was warm and the grip was strong. "You too."

"Good! Good!" Charlotte pushed them together with a hand on each of their backs. "Get acquainted. We'll have a speed through here any minute."

When she scurried off, Keith was left struggling for something to say.

"You'll get used to her." Carl's eyes darted to his director. "Her energy level drains the shit out of me."

Keith laughed shyly.

"What else have you done?" Carl asked, his voice deep and masculine.

"Not a lot. To be honest, this is my debut. I did mostly commercials, and even those I haven't done in a year."

"Well, this is your big break, Keith. It's done wonders for my career. The show is top rated, the writing is fantastic, and they are on the cutting edge of cable television drama."

"I know. I've watched the show and been a fan of the whole first season. I love it."

"Good. That helps." Carl smiled.

Keith found himself staring at Carl's lips. He felt he had to. He was going to have to kiss this man. Standing next to him, feeling some hot aura of sexuality emanating from him, Keith wondered if his fears were worse than reality. After all, the guy was unbelievable looking. It could be worse. He could be kissing an ugly geek or an old man.

"Have you reviewed the script?" Carl asked.

"Yes. I've got my part memorized. I didn't want to fuck up the first day."

"Wow. Good job. It's rough for me. I don't know why. Once I get going I'm okay, but I have to admit I sometimes write cues on my hand."

Seeing Carl's sweet expression, Keith felt so much more at ease than he had five minutes ago. The guy was down to earth, not cocky or conceited.

"I just hope my nerves don't get the best of me."

"Don't worry. No one here is nasty. It's a good, patient group. I love working with them, and I pray this drama keeps going for years like some of the other hits they've had."

"You do? You really like the job?"

"Are you kidding me? It's steady work. And last season I was a relatively minor player. With your character on board, we'll both be getting some of the best scenes."

A flutter washed through Keith's gut. It was a mix of anxiety and delight. More scenes? More homosexual scenes? Could he ever get used to that?

Charlotte's booming shout carried over the noise. "Let's do a speed read! Where are my boys?"

"That's us." Carl nodded to the stage area.

As Keith made his way behind him, he hoped he didn't fall on his face.

"Right. You need a copy of the script, blondie?" Charlotte addressed Keith.

"No. I've got it."

"Good boy! Listen up everyone! Our newest star has his script memorized already. Learn from him." She smiled at Keith. "I'm teasing you." She rushed away as Keith inspected the familiar set of a living room in the main family's house.

Battling his nerves, Keith rehearsed his lines in his head as Charlotte gave him and Carl a quick idea of what she wanted from them.

"You just met, boys. Troy, Dennis is the brother of your best friend."

Keith was trying to get used to her using their character names. This was all so new to him he hoped he didn't get stage fright.

"Let's see what you can do." She sat down and waited. "Begin."

9

Carl began the dialogue, "Dennis, Xavier told me you're in trouble."

Keith forced himself to become his character. "I am. I'm sunk. My brother has been singing your praises. He said you're the best lawyer in the city."

"He's right."

"Can you help me?"

Carl paused, doing a deliberate appraisal of Keith's body. It was so sensual Keith felt the goose bumps rise on his skin.

"I think I can," Carl crooned.

Moving closer to him, Keith touched Carl's arm. "I'm serious, Troy. If you can't make this problem go away, I don't know what I will do."

Looking down at the contact, Carl gave Keith an adoring smile. "You just let me handle it. I owe it to Xavier to get you off the hook."

"Thanks, Troy. I mean that. I don't have too much money…"

Carl cupped Keith's face. Keith's skin went icy and his heart began going berserk under his chest.

"You don't worry about money, Dennis. We'll work something out."

"Cut! Perfect! Oh, the chemistry between you two is amazing," Charlotte cheered.

Keith stepped back from Carl, trying to regain his composure. What the hell was that all about? His body was going wild. He'd become a complete shivering bundle of nerves. Checking to see if Carl showed any reaction to the scene, he found him reading over the script, looking very casual. Continuing to back away from the crowd as the next scene was about to be read, Keith fought to control himself. He was trembling in spasms of fear.

Standing outside the set, Keith crossed his arms over his chest tightly. This was what he was waiting for, wasn't it? This huge break into the world of acting? What the hell was he going to tell his mother and father? Hi, Mom, Dad, I play a fag on TV.

They would understand, wouldn't they? They knew ever since he was in high school drama club he had aimed for an acting career. They even paid for his singing lessons. Sent him to USC's drama school. They were one hundred percent behind him. But…

Jesus. Why this? Couldn't I play some macho sports hunk on daytime soaps? Not a fag for a racy cable television series.

Charlotte was beckoning for him to step up to the plate once

10

more.

Clearing his throat, Keith hurried back to her.

"Right, next scene. You two ready?"

Keith nodded.

"Good." She crossed her arms waiting. "On your own time..."

Inhaling deeply, Keith tried to relax as Carl held aloft the paperwork in his hand.

"Ready?" Keith whispered.

"Yes."

Trying to focus, Keith inhaled to calm himself and began. "It's blackmail, Troy. Plain and simple. I just don't know if I should go to the police without a lawyer with me."

"You did the right thing, Dennis."

"Will you come to the station with me?"

Carl rested his hand on Keith's shoulder. It sent Keith's body into another trembling fit. Tensing his muscles he tried to fight it.

"Why don't we discuss what really happened first?" Carl rubbed him softly.

Almost forgetting his line, Keith forced himself to look into Carl's green eyes. "Yes. I need to tell you everything."

"You do. It's the only way I can help you."

"I'll do anything you need me to do, Troy."

"I know, Dennis. I'm not worried about that."

Keith stared at Carl as if they were waiting for someone to say something. Finally, Keith whispered, "Isn't that it?"

"I think so." Carl read over the paper he was holding.

Waiting, looking at Charlotte and the rest of the crew, Keith asked, "Was it all right?"

"Yes. Perfect." Charlotte paced and added, "I don't want the scene to end there. Why don't we keep them going?"

As Charlotte and company debated, Keith sat down on a chair, interlocked his fingers, resting them on his lap, watching. Carl sat next to him and leaned on his shoulder to whisper, "This is when the quick reads turn into hours."

Keith gave a soft chuckle.

"You're doing really well, Keith. I can tell you have some good training."

"Thanks, Carl."

After another silent pause, Carl said softly, "Christ, why don't they just decide. I hate waiting around."

"Does it happen often?"

"Sometimes Charlotte begins brainstorming and changing things around. I get very frustrated."

"That's her job." When Keith turned to look, Carl was smiling wryly at him. "What?"

"It'll get on your nerves. I promise."

Charlotte turned back to address them. "Look, let's keep going through the next scene. This one's too short and I don't like where it breaks."

"Okay." Keith sat up on the chair.

"Right. Take it from 'I'm not worried about that'."

Turning back to stare at Carl, Keith waited for his next line. As Carl spoke, Keith focused on Carl's mouth and eyes, forcing himself to repeat his rehearsed lines and not get distracted.

By the time he arrived at his apartment, Keith was exhausted. Parking in front of the building, he took the new script with revisions penciled in up to his unit. When he walked through the door, the apartment was vacant. Patty's waitress job was for mostly nights and weekends.

Tossing the script down on the kitchen counter, Keith took a beer out of the fridge. He twisted off the top, taking a deep draw off of it. Leaning back against the Formica counter, Keith had his character's lines spinning in his head. Charlotte's suggestions, ideas, and motivations were overlapping the words he was reading. It was overwhelming. They didn't have long to prepare. It was a weekly series and they needed to get the lines and directions down quickly. Walking around the living room with the beer connected to his mouth and his revised script in his hand elevated at eye level, Keith memorized the changes, hiding the text and saying the lines.

A strange flash of nerves washed over him.

Carl's hand resting on his shoulder came back like a vision or dream. It wasn't in the script. Nowhere in the script did it say, "Troy Wright now touches Dennis Jason's shoulder."

"Get used to it, Keith. You're going to get a lot more contact from Carl than that," he mumbled. As if suddenly he had to prove his manhood to himself, he set the bottle and script down and dialed Patty's number.

She sounded rushed.

"Sorry. I know you're busy." He felt bad.

"Yes. You okay? How did it go?"

"Good. I just wanted to say hi. See you later."

"Okay. Bye!" She hung up.

He set the phone down and walked to the window looking out across the street to the apartment house opposite theirs. Though his gut was in knots, he knew this was a good thing for his career. He had no choice.

Turning to walk to the bathroom, Keith flipped on the light and looked at himself in the mirror. Brushing his hand back through his blond hair, the echo of Adam's comment about him being too pretty reverberated in his head. He leaned his hands on the sink and studied his eyes and facial features. "I'm not fucking pretty. Bullshit. I look like a guy."

Parting the buttons of his shirt, he opened it up and stood back, inspecting his appearance. His chest was well developed, though almost hairless. But that was genetics. His parents were both blue-eyed blonds, and his dad's hair was so fair you could hardly see it on his arms and legs.

"Fuck you, Adam. I am not pretty."

He flicked off the light and returned to fetch his beer, brooding.

Lying in bed and watching TV, Keith heard the door and checked the time. Hopping out of the covers to greet Patty, Keith found her taking off her jacket and setting her purse on the kitchen table.

"Hey."

"Hi." She appeared tired.

"Are you hungry?"

"No. I ate at the restaurant. I just want to shower and sleep."

He stepped back as she passed him by to the bedroom.

"How did your first day go?"

As she took off her uniform, Keith leaned against the doorframe. "Good."

"Are the actors cool?"

"Yes. They're really nice."

"You're so lucky, Keith. I wish I could get a break like that."

He followed her to the bathroom as she finished taking off her undergarments. "You will."

"I doubt it. I don't have Adam Lewis as my agent." Reaching into the shower, she turned on the water, waiting as it heated up.

Staring at her naked body, Keith wanted them to make love before they slept. Patty was very slim, almost too skinny. Her shoulder blades poked out of her back in sharp angels, and her bottom was flat.

He had answered her ad to share an apartment. Originally he didn't think they would connect on any kind of deep level, but he was a man and she was a woman, and it just happened one night after some beers.

The apartment had two bedrooms, but Patty stayed in his now.

When she stepped into the shower to wash, Keith reached into his briefs, touching his cock. He wasn't hard, but could motivate himself if he tried.

"So," Patty asked over the noise of running water, "what was it like?"

"It was good."

"Good? That's it? What's Carl Bronson like? He's really cute."

"He's nice. He seems pretty down to earth." Keith's fondling of his own cock was getting it hard. When an intruding thought of Carl's hand on his him popped into his mind, Keith forced himself to stare at Patty's blurry naked form to get it out.

She turned off the water and wrung out her black hair. When she opened the door to reach for a towel, she moaned, "Oh, no way. Keith, I'm exhausted."

Taking his hand out of his briefs, Keith shrugged. "It's okay."

She stepped out of the tub and vigorously dried her hair, Patty said softly, "Sorry. I know we don't make love very often."

"I understand. The job wears you out. I suppose soon mine will as well." His cock quickly lost its erection.

Watching her comb through her wet hair, seeing her small, but firm, breasts in the mirror's reflection, Keith lowered his eyes. "I'll be waiting in bed for you."

"Okay. I'll be there in a minute."

Heading back to the bed, Keith shut off the television with the remote, and climbed under the sheets waiting.

He couldn't understand his melancholy mood. He'd been accepted into the hottest new series on cable, and finally had something to brag about. Why did he still feel so lost?

Rolling to his back, staring at the wall with the bookcase and small portable television wedged into one of the shelves, Keith knew what his fears were, and that haunting sense of dread was blocking the euphoria he should be feeling.

Patty emerged from the bathroom and slipped on a small, loose fitting shorts and tank top pajama set. She snuggled under the covers, her back to him and mumbled, "Goodnight, Keith."

"Night."

He reached for the light on the nightstand and turned it off. As he lay in the darkness, hearing Patty's deep breathing quickly plunging her into sleep, Keith's heart ached.

Chapter Two

Carl sipped his cup of black coffee in his new condominium. Standing out on the terrace, the view of the city and surrounding hills visible through the smog, he repeated his lines in his head to get them embedded in his brain cells. Tiny flashes of excitement kept sparking through him. He loved the fact that his character's popularity had grown and his initially small part was expanding. Fan sites had begun to pop up on the web. He had waited his whole life for that. At thirty he felt slightly old to be just beginning his prime in acting. Previously living in New York and doing nothing but theater and stage work, Carl truly felt vindicated to all the doubting family members who told him he would never make it. Acting for a living was like a game of roulette, and almost everyone went home from the casino empty handed.

Landing the role as Troy Wright was like winning the lottery.

But…

Carl wondered if this new direction, this sudden gay storyline was good or bad for his career.

Stepping back into his kitchen, Carl checked the time and refilled his cup. The upcoming season was supposed to twist and turn the plot of Forever Young to astound the viewers. The one thing Charlotte Deavers did not want was predictability. And from the start of the show, Carl's character, Troy Wright, had given no indication of his sexuality. He had actually been asexual, not making a move either way. Carl had always thought that was strange. But now he knew why they had kept his preference ambiguous. They must have had his character in mind for being gay from the beginning, though they never mentioned it to him before. Receiving the new script, seeing where they were taking him, Carl was very apprehensive and nervous. Though he had to admit the thought of touching a man had crossed his mind previously, Carl hadn't acted on it.

Gay men surrounded him in drama school, but none struck his fancy enough to accept their propositions.

Carl thought it was ironic he wasn't dating women either. Life imitating art, he was becoming his character.

A brief fling with one of the female technical staff of Forever Young that went nowhere was his only sexual foray in ages. He told himself it was because he was busy. Too busy to date. And the idea of going through a "dating" game to find a mate didn't really fill him with enthusiasm.

The irony was that very soon he was going to be acting gay and in bed with a man.

An image of Keith O'Leary came to mind. The man was so damn adorable. He hadn't even imagined asking Keith if he was gay or had an opinion of the role they were going to play. He didn't know Keith well enough, and knew if someone had asked him that question he didn't know how he would answer it.

It was a job. They went to work, did what they were paid to do, and came home. Wasn't that the reality?

Carl had no idea what kissing Keith would be like, and he dreaded and craved it simultaneously. Why he craved it worried him.

To himself he whispered, "You just crave human touch, Carl. That's the damn problem."

Happy to be back on the set, Keith was escorted to a room with clothing hanging on metal racks. His wardrobe assistant stood near, pushing loaded hangers across the metal poles. Melvin held a shirt against Keith's chest.

"Yes. Perfect with your eyes."

Keith felt slightly uncomfortable by the man's obvious feminine lisp.

"Try this one. And these black slacks."

Keith looked around the room.

"Oh, don't turn modest on me, Keith-dear. Before long you'll be stripped down for your sex scenes."

Wanting to tell Mel to shut up, Keith instead took off his shirt and jeans.

As he slipped the clothing on, he caught Melvin's gaze on his crotch. "Come on, man," Keith whined, "use a little tact?"

"Get used to it, honey. With your looks and body, you'll be on every internet gay site the minute the new series starts."

Feeling sick to his stomach at that thought, Keith stepped into the slacks and zipped up the fly.

Melvin checked the fit. "Not bad. Go, take a look." He pointed to a triple mirror.

Walking towards it, Keith brushed his hair back from his forehead and inspected the clothing.

Another shirt in his hand, Melvin held it up under Keith's chin. "No. Light blue. It has to be light blue for this scene." Melvin twisted around, shouting out, "Ken!"

Another man showed up behind Keith in the mirror's reflection.

"He's ready for you."

"Great." Ken tapped Keith's arm. "This way."

Sitting in a chair having a man apply powder to his face and brush his hair, Keith imagined all the contact from the male employees was prepping him for the ultimate performance. Of course that was just something he thought of on his own. It was silly, but it was a way to stop flinching every time a man laid his hands on him.

Patty hadn't budged this morning when he woke. He had tried to cuddle behind her, his morning hard-on hungry for release. She just groaned in exhaustion and edged away.

Keith thought their relationship was unusual. When he first met her, answering her ad, he didn't think she was his type. But as the living arrangements encouraged them to lose their modesty between each other, Keith began to think of Patty like a sister. Until she made a pass.

They were watching TV and a passionate love scene from a late night movie had flipped her switch. When she offered, Keith accepted. But in retrospect he wondered if it wasn't a mistake and the brother and sister respect they had once had should have been maintained. Sex complicated life. He didn't mind getting his rocks off with her on occasion, but he knew Patty wasn't his ideal match.

Keith still felt too young to be thinking about being tied down, and at times resented Patty for her possessiveness. Yet at other moments, he appreciated her help and advice.

He was woken out of his thoughts by someone calling his name. Ken removed his paper make-up shield from his shirt and stood back.

"Thanks." Keith hurried off, jogging to the set.

Seeing Carl in his character's clothing, looking polished and fresh, Keith felt a tiny flutter of nerves race through him.

Charlotte urged Keith to come over to her. He did and leaned down closer, as it seemed as if she wanted to whisper something to him.

"You ever kiss a man, cutie?"

"No, ma'am," he laughed nervously.

"Well, I'm afraid you're going to get your chance." She looked over Keith's shoulder for a moment before continuing. "Close your eyes and pretend it's a woman if you need to. But you are going to have to get used to it."

"I know." Keith stomach tied in knots.

"Whatever you do, try not to recoil in disgust. It'll really upset the gay employees."

Chuckling, though he was wrought with nerves, Keith replied, "I won't. Promise."

"Okay, babe. Knock 'em dead."

Meeting Carl on the set, Keith smiled at him.

"You get the pep talk?" Carl asked.

"Yes. Did you?"

"I did. Something about not acting grossed out. What does she expect us to do, spit and wipe our tongues on our sleeve?"

Keith looked back at Charlotte as Carl's eyes seemed to find her in the group. Clearing his throat, Keith asked, "Uh, have you ever kissed a guy before, Carl?"

"No."

That made Keith feel a whole lot better.

"You?"

"Nope." Keith shifted side to side nervously.

"I really think they're making too much of it. I can't see how it could be such a big deal with the kind of movies they have in theaters nowadays."

"You're right. I have to admit I was getting myself worked up about it."

"Don't. It's not worth it, Keith. It's two seconds in the shot."

"Yes, it is, isn't it?" Keith's nerves settled down. He touched Carl's arm through his suit jacket. "Thanks. I mean it."

"Don't worry about it."

Both of them stood waiting as Charlotte answered some

technical questions from her crew.

Finally she addressed them. "All right. Let's get this going. You guys ready?"

Keith nodded, turning to see Carl giving her the same indication.

"Okay, this is our camera rehearsal. Let's get quiet on the set!"

Keith relaxed his arms to his sides and looked at Carl who was staring at him with the same intensity.

"Living room scene. Take one! Action!" was shouted and the surroundings became dead quiet.

"Thanks, Troy. I mean that. I don't have too much money..." Keith said, waiting for Carl's line.

Carl cupped Keith's face. Even with Carl's reassurances Keith felt his body become a bag of nerves.

"You don't worry about money, Dennis. We'll work something out."

Keith swallowed down his dry throat. "But I don't know what else I can offer you."

"Don't you?" Carl purred.

"You...you mean..." Keith felt his skin cover in goose bumps.

"I find you very attractive, Dennis."

"But, Troy, I'm not, you know..." Keith tried not to flinch as Carl cupped his jaw with both hands.

"First kiss me, then tell me that."

Knowing it was coming, Keith closed his eyes. Carl's lips brushed gently over his. Keith felt as if he were about to pass out from humiliation knowing so many people were watching them.

Carl parted slowly from the contact.

Opening his eyes, seeing the kindness in Carl's face, and knowing that wasn't an act, Keith felt slightly less freaked out.

"Well?" Carl smiled. "Still need convincing?"

"No. It's a deal." Keith breathed, panting from the nerves and wishing he wasn't.

Carl caressed Keith's hair affectionately. "I knew you would see it my way."

Keith smiled at him in reflex, not knowing if that was appropriate.

Charlotte shouted, "Cut!" followed by, "Beautiful, boys. Absolutely beautiful. Okay, let's check out what we have." She headed back to a monitor.

Keith moved away from Carl, trying not to make eye contact with him because his cheeks were hot and he knew that meant they were red. There was some commotion about lighting and sound in the background. Carl mumbled, "You ready to do it again?"

Keith looked up at the group. "How many times do you think we'll repeat the scene?"

"Who knows? After the camera rehearsals, one or two times? Hell, she's a perfectionist and it's her budget."

Waiting for someone to tell them what to do, he and Carl stood idly by until the adjustments were made.

"Sorry. Where were we? Let's do it again." Charlotte relaxed in her chair. "Ready?"

Someone shouted, "Living room scene. Take two! Action!"

Repeating the same dialogue, Keith felt like the ice had been broken somewhat between he and Carl. His shaking had subsided and he wasn't as terrified of the kiss. Well, it was barely a kiss at all in his opinion. He couldn't remember the last time he did nothing but brush his closed lips against a woman's. He preferred a more sensuous version. Keith wondered if eventually, as this television relationship evolved, if they would be expected to open their mouths when they did it. Trying not to feel nervous about it, he decided he'd cross that bridge when he came to it.

Carl just wanted the damn scene completed. How many times was he supposed to kiss this guy? Trying to get into character, shaking off his annoyance, Carl resumed his position on the stage.

Running over the same dialogue again, Carl cupped Keith's face and noticed he appeared considerably less nervous this time.

"First kiss me, then tell me that," Carl echoed the rehearsed line. Reaching up his other hand to urge Keith to his mouth, Carl lightly caressed Keith's lips with his own, parting and staring into Keith's face. "Well?" Carl smiled. "Still need convincing?"

It was a pretty harmless scene as far as Carl was concerned. Since this was cable television, Carl had a feeling this was only the beginning of the on screen love affair, and truly had no clue how it would feel to do simulated sex scenes with Keith, or to even kiss him with more passion.

When he had asked Charlotte about the coming episodes, she

had given him a vague reply, something about wanting to keep the plot fresh and not having too many advanced scripts to peruse.

Was that really it? Or was she afraid of someone getting cold feet? Carl had asked himself how far he would be willing to go for his career. Nudity? Front? Back? What?

He didn't know. His agent promised him even if his bottom was shown on television, naked and exposed, it would be a boost to his career.

Carl assumed everyone with a cut of his paycheck would want him to agree to anything. So he didn't take anyone's advice by his own.

"Well done, boys. Take a break."

Carl tapped Keith on the shoulder, gesturing to a refreshment table set up with soft drinks.

After getting them each a bottle of ice water, Carl asked, "You survive?"

A soft nervous chuckle preempted Keith's response. "I did. It was pretty benign."

"I thought so as well, but don't get too comfortable thinking that's going to be the extent of it."

"No. I agree. I've seen some of the other shows that were on television with gay characters. Some of them can get pretty racy."

Carl looked around the area first, gesturing for Keith to walk away from the few people who lingered. "How much have you been told about the upcoming storyline?"

"Not a lot." Keith sipped the water. "Just two guys in a relationship, why?"

Taking another scan quickly, Carl whispered, "I have a feeling it's going to be cranked up to another level very soon."

"Shit. Really? After barely a peck on the lips?"

"You remember that series, Ties That Bind?"

"Yes. It dabbled in some sexual bondage, but it never really showed much whipping or torture."

"That was Charlotte's." Seeing Keith's expression, Carl added, "Did you know that?"

"No. It was on ages ago."

"Not that long ago. Only two years or so."

"Is she going to turn this drama into some S and M fantasy?" Keith laughed.

"No. I doubt it. That's not what I'm getting at. Do you recall the sex scenes in it?"

"Hell yeah. They were fucking hot." Keith took another sip of his water. "But they were between a man and a woman."

"That show was getting non-stop publicity for its nudity. Remember?" He paused, waiting for Keith to get the picture.

"But..." Keith shook his head.

Nodding, Carl replied, "Yes. She will."

"No one shows a man's dick on television."

"You wait."

"Yours or mine?" Keith gasped.

"Flip a coin." Carl peeked back at the action, making sure they weren't needed.

"Holy crap. You know, Carl, I haven't even told my parents I got this role."

"You'd better. If they find out from reading the gossip columns they'll be pissed off."

"No one ever said I was expected to be naked. I'm not very happy about that."

"No one's said it to me either, Keith. But that doesn't mean it's not hanging out there." Pausing, Carl realized his pun and started laughing.

Keith caught it immediately and joined him.

"Shit. I didn't mean it to come out like that." Carl dabbed at a tear in his eye.

"I know what you meant." Keith fought to control his laughter. "Look, Carl, I imagined the usual. You know, some scenes in a bed where we had no shirts on. I really didn't expect more than that."

"What bothers me is that they won't give me advanced scripts." Carl finished his water and crushed his plastic bottle in his hand.

"Is that unusual?"

"Yes and no. Sometimes the writers just go with the flow, others have the entire series mapped out. Charlotte tends to allow the characters to evolve."

"Then don't imagine it as sinister, Carl. And why are you asking me about what's going to happen? You've been doing this for one season already. I'm the new guy."

"I know. I just can't help but wonder if they told you these things up front to prepare you."

"No. My agent told me it was a gay character. That was it."

Nodding, Carl replied, "Just hold onto your hat when this

show begins rolling to mid-season sweeps."

Someone was calling their names. They returned, tossing out their empty bottles and taped the final scene of the episode. It was just dialogue so Carl didn't think much about it, until he was given the next script.

Keith drove home, the new episode sitting next to him on the passenger's seat. Parking, knowing Patty was at work, he entered the building, jogged up the stairs and through his front door. Once he had a beer in his fist, he sat down on the couch and began reading.

Skipping passed the scenes he was not in, Keith slowed down at his and Carl's dialogue, noting the action in parentheses. Sucking on the beer, imagining the details, Keith choked and reread the paragraph. "Fuck. Carl was right. Jesus! Already?" His heart beginning to pound in his ribcage, Keith set the script aside to recover. "I don't believe this."

Resting his beer on the coffee table, checking the time, Keith picked up the phone and dialed.

"Hello?"

"Adam? I hope it's not too late."

"No. Not at all. How'd the first episode go?"

"It was fine. No problems. Look, when you sent me on that audition, did you realize I would have to do some nude scenes?"

A pause followed before Adam replied, "I didn't get anything specific from them. I figured since it's a cable drama, there may be some slight nudity. Why?"

"I'm sitting here with the script on my lap for the second episode, and I'm already supposed to be naked."

"I wouldn't worry, Keith. It'll be shot either from the back or something will block the view of your dick."

"Are you sure?"

"No one shows a man frontally nude. Not on cable. There are very few exceptions, Keith."

"Carl thinks Charlotte Deavers wants something shocking for February sweeps."

"What do you want me to do, Keith?"

That shut Keith up. He didn't know the answer to that question. "I just wanted to know if someone advised you I would be doing nude scenes."

"The answer to that question is no. All they said was that it was a gay romance. That was it. You want to quit?"

"No. I just think it would have been nice to have been forewarned."

"Would it have made you reconsider?"

Again, Keith didn't know the answer. "I'm not sure."

"Do you just want me to reassure you? Is that what you're looking for?"

Did he?

"Yes. Yes, Adam. Maybe that's what I want."

"Okay, look, Keith…you are in the best…the best new drama series in cable history. The amount of good, and even controversial, publicity this show is creating is already making each and every star a household name. You know that guy who plays Xavier? Omar Desmond? He's already been cast in a big movie production. The guy has no other credentials on his resume but Forever Young."

"Good. Very good."

"Is that what you wanted to hear?"

"Yes."

"Did you have to kiss Carl yet? Is that why you're so freaked out?"

"We did, but it wasn't even a real kiss. It was just his mouth brushing against mine."

"You sound disappointed."

Keith could hear the amusement in his voice. "Funny, Adam."

"I've got to go. But call me whenever you need a pep talk. I'm here."

"Thanks, Adam."

"I'm dying to see the first new episode."

Laughing, Keith answered, "I bet you are. You get off on men kissing."

"You said it! See ya, Keith."

"Bye." Keith hung up, smiling. Setting the phone back down, he kept reading the script, the expression falling from his face.

When Patty finally arrived home, Keith had most of his lines already memorized. It was something he prided himself on. He didn't have trouble with the dialogue like some actors tended to.

"Hello?"

"Hi, Patty," he shouted to her.

She poked her head into the bedroom. "New script?"

"Yes."

As she shed her uniform she asked, "And?"

"It's top secret. You have to keep your mouth shut. No gossip around the kitchen at work."

"Really?"

"Really."

"I'll wait. I don't want it to spoil the show for me."

She disappeared into the bathroom. Keith heard the shower start soon after. Setting the script on the floor, Keith slipped off his briefs and pushed the blankets to his knees. He wanted to make love. There was something about the upcoming scenes with Carl that compelled Keith to reaffirm his manhood. And in his mind, that meant screwing a woman.

Digging into the nightstand for a condom, Keith set it out within reach and began masturbating to get hard. As he did, flashes of the action in the script kept popping into his head. It began getting him irritated. Cursing at himself, he climbed out of bed and entered the steamy bathroom, staring at Patty's nakedness behind the blurry shower doors.

"Keith?"

"Yeah."

"I'm really wiped out."

"You say that every night, Patty."

"I know but I am. I'm on my feet for nine hours."

"Can't you just lie there? I'll do all the work."

"No. Please?"

"Jesus, Patty. Why do we even sleep in the same room?"

She shut off the water and pushed back the door. "I thought you liked sleeping together."

"I'd like to have sex once in a while."

"We do. That's not fair, Keith."

His body deflating as she stepped out of the tub and dried off, Keith asked, "When? When was the last time?"

"I don't keep count. Do you?"

"Never mind." He left the bathroom and burrowed under the sheets again, feeling frustrated. He had to find a willing woman or his frail ego would fall apart.

Chapter Three

Carl choked as he read the script. Sitting at his kitchen table, munching a piece of toast for breakfast, Carl shook his head in awe. "I knew it. Christ, Charlotte, you didn't waste any time. The second episode? Holy shit." Carl sipped his coffee, his eyes glued to the written words. "Keith. You did it to Keith. That poor schmuck." Carl wished he had Keith's phone number. He reminded himself to ask for it. They had to talk about this and there wasn't much privacy on the set.

"Oh well, you want ratings, Charlotte? This will get you viewers, but I don't know about accolades."

Carl finished his breakfast and cleared the dishes. Hurrying, he grabbed his keys and locked his condo, jogging to the elevator and then the garage. Opening the car door with a remote control, he climbed into his Corvette and started the engine, heading to the studio.

On the drive there he tried to remember some of the lines he had read, but also thought about the next scenes he and Keith were about to do. If it was making Carl nervous, it must be driving Keith insane.

"Bet the poor guy didn't sleep a wink last night." Carl entered the studio lot, showing his ID at the gate.

Once he had parked, dashing across the busy parking lot, Carl made his way to the set and looked for Keith. He found him sitting on a folding chair, reading the script.

Pulling up a chair beside him, Carl asked, "You okay?"

Keith gave him a pained look.

"Give me your mobile number. I wanted to call you to talk about it but couldn't."

Before Keith opened his mouth to reply, Carl grabbed someone to borrow a pen and paper. Once they had exchanged information, Carl waved the assistant away. Staring down at the script on Keith's lap, Carl asked, "Will you do it?"

"What the hell choice do I have?"

"You always have a choice, Keith. Sit Charlotte down and tell her you won't."

Keith gave a sarcastic, choking laugh.

"You want me to say something?"

"No. I've reread that scene a hundred times. I spoke to my agent, and he said just because I'm nude doesn't mean they'll show my dick on the television."

"True. But how do you feel about being in the buff in front of the cast and crew? Are you that confident? If you are, I envy you."

"I'm not ashamed of my body. But I have to admit I'm slightly anxious about being the only one naked in the room."

"I can fake it. I'm under the damn sheets."

"I know." Keith flipped pages to the scene in question. "Look, it says I take off my clothes and stand facing you, then I climb in with you. So? It's got to be a back view."

"That would be my assumption."

Keith shrugged. "Then it'll be a quick shot of my ass. Big deal."

"Really? You're that okay with it?"

Exhaling in frustration, Keith hissed, "What the hell am I supposed to do if I'm not, Carl? I'm brand fucking new. If I start screwing with Charlotte now, she'll write me out by the next episode. I need the money. I have to keep going."

Without a thought, Carl pushed a strand of blond hair back from Keith's eyes. "I hear you. Really, I do. If and when it's my turn, I'll just grit my teeth and bear it. Literally."

Keith was staring at him strangely.

"What?" Carl asked curiously. Suddenly he realized he had touched Keith. "Oh. I'm sorry. I don't know why I did that. I feel like an idiot. It was just hanging over your eye." Carl went crimson. "Christ, that was really forward of me. I'm sorry, Keith."

"No. It's all right. I suppose the more comfortable we are with each other the easier this will be."

Carl began beating himself up internally. Why on earth did he do that? Since he felt like a complete imbecile, Carl stood off the chair to escape. "I'll let you finish."

"Thanks."

Walking away, Carl tried to find a corner to hide in. What the hell was he thinking reaching out and touching Keith like that? Was it a good thing he felt so relaxed around Keith? Or was it something else?

Keith stood alongside Carl as they watched two other characters going through their lines. Keith knew they were up next for blocking. It was just a read through to get directions, so he didn't have to peel off his clothing just yet. Or at least he didn't think he would have to.

Charlotte beckoned them to the stage which was the set of Carl's bedroom. Fully clothed, Carl climbed on the bed with the script in his hand.

"Okay, Keith, Dennis knows this is payment for services, so he's slightly apprehensive."

Nodding, Keith was glad because that's exactly how he felt in reality.

"But as soon as your two bodies collide between the sheets, it's magical. Got it?"

"Yes."

"Need a script or prompt?"

"No."

"I love you! Christ, people, the new guy already has the stuff memorized. He's making you all look bad." She winked to soften the tease. "When you're ready, sweetie."

Focusing on Carl's expression of sincere support as he lay on the bed waiting, Keith began pretending to take off his clothing. "I hope it's enough for you, Troy."

"Will it ever be enough?" Carl read from the script, looking back at Keith.

"It better be. You can't expect me to keep whoring for you eternally." Keith mimed stepping out of his pants.

"Whoring? Is that what you're doing?"

"Sex as payment? What do you call it?" Keith was supposedly naked now, so he faced Carl, his hands on his hips.

"I call it love," Carl mocked.

"Love?"

Carl craned his finger at him. "Get over here. Now."

As Carl animated lifting up the covers, Keith pretended to crawl under them.

They scooted down on the bed, facing each other.

31

"You know I think you're incredibly handsome," Carl purred, stroking Keith's hair back from his face. "And judging by your hard-on, the feeling must be mutual."

"It's only hard because it's been a long time since I've had release."

"And I have to ask myself why." Carl continued to stroke Keith's hair.

It was relaxing Keith so much he fought to concentrate.

"You know why. You know what I've been dealing with. That woman is blackmailing me."

"Because?" Carl leaned closer, almost to Keith's lips.

Keith's pulse skyrocketed, his breathing was getting impossible to control. "Because…I've been with a man."

"Precisely," Carl agreed.

As Carl drew nearer, about to touch lips, Keith's heart was pumping so hard it was making noise in his eardrums.

Charlotte's voice commanded, "Fine! You've already made love…move to the scene after when you're lying back on the pillows."

Keith dropped to his back, staring at the lights suspended from the ceiling. His body was so wound up he was in pain. How on earth was he supposed to do this naked?

Paper rattled and Carl found his place on the script. "See? That wasn't so bad, was it?"

"No…" Keith panted. "Not bad at all."

Carl crawled over to rest on Keith's chest. "I could really let myself go with a man like you."

"Don't count on it being permanent. Think about it, Troy. My damn lawyer is protecting me from a blackmailer, while using me for sex. Do you think I'm doing this because I want to?"

"You want to." Carl stroked Keith's chest.

Keith suspected Carl could feel his pounding heart. He'd have to be numb not to.

Twisting around to face him, Keith cupped Carl's jaw, feeling the stiffness of the shadow of his beard. It felt as foreign to him as Saturn's moons. "You're right. I lied. I've wanted you ever since my brother brought you to our house for dinner five years ago. I just never knew you felt the same way."

"I do, Dennis. I was just afraid to tell you."

"And now?"

"Now? I'm no longer married and I'm free to be myself."

Keith knew they were supposed to kiss again here, but they didn't. "Can I tell you a secret?"

"Of course."

"I've always loved you."

"That's not a secret," Carl laughed seductively. "That, my handsome lover, is a fact."

The next act was an embrace, and the end of the scene.

Charlotte shouted, "You two are so fantastic! I can't wait to see this tomorrow for camera rehearsal."

Keith knew she meant without their clothing on and with all the action in place. Climbing off the bed, he felt as if he needed a shot of brandy he was trembling so badly.

Sensing someone behind him as he filled a cup with juice, Keith looked over his shoulder at Carl.

"You okay?"

"Yeah." Keith nodded, gulping the juice.

"I felt you trembling."

"Shit. I'm sorry."

"Don't worry. I doubt it was noticeable."

"Wish I had fucking booze."

A low chuckle rumbled from Carl's chest. He opened a bottle of mineral water and sipped it. "Don't get into that habit. See that woman over there?"

Keith asked, "Betty? The lady who plays your mother?"

"Yup. She's into the booze every shoot. Keeps it in her bra or something, I don't fucking know. But she reeks."

"Ew, nice."

"You don't have any scenes with her yet. When you do, she'll drive you crazy. She never remembers her damn lines. I think the only reason they have her on is for nostalgia. She was in some sitcom in the seventies and Charlotte loves using the old timers to get the boomers interested."

Keith finished his juice and poured more.

"Why don't you sit down?"

"Christ, do I look that bad?" Keith hoped no one else noticed.

"You have to expect to be nervous, Keith. I was the same during my first couple of episodes. And I wasn't naked and expected to kiss a guy then. I've had a season to get used to it."

Keith sat down on a folding chair. Carl relaxed in the one next to him leaning over his lap as he looked at the stage and the next scene being run through.

"Can I call you?"

Carl sat up and met Keith's eyes. "Of course."

"I mean, just to talk over the lines."

"I know what you mean."

"How late do you go to bed?"

"Around eleven or twelve. I spend most of the evening memorizing."

"Maybe we could read together, over the phone."

"We could do that."

Keith wondered if he was beginning to sound like he was insecure. Well hell, he was a little. "Are you sure you don't mind?"

"I'm sure." Carl gave him a warm smile. "If I were you, I'd be asking for some moral support right about now as well."

"My fucking parents have no idea." Keith lowered his voice. "I don't know how to tell them."

"Keith! You're not coming out to them." Carl tried not to laugh.

"Almost. My dad will see it as the same damn thing."

"Oh, come on." Carl shook his head at the thought. "It's a job, Keith. A good job that pays well."

"Did your parents react at all when you said you were playing a gay man?"

"I wasn't originally. The whole first season my sexuality was kept up in the air. I suppose I should have known. When a main character doesn't have a girlfriend? Nowadays that only means one thing."

"So? What did they say when you told them about this season?"

Carl's cheeks went crimson.

At his shy expression, Keith burst out laughing and was told to shush by someone near the set. He covered his mouth and whispered, "You didn't tell them either."

"No. Not yet. Hell, the stupid show doesn't air for another month or so. I figured I had some time."

Smiling at Carl's modesty, Keith never would have thought a guy who was so popular on a hit series like this would be so cool. It was such a relief to have him there. If Carl were a snob, full of himself, or unfriendly, Keith didn't know how he would have handled the difficulty of such a demanding role.

"Thanks."

"For what?" Carl asked.

"For being so nice."

"Christ, Keith, we can't hate each other. Tomorrow we'll be climbing all over each other in bed."

A shiver raced down Keith's spine. He assumed it had to be from nerves. "At least you get to wear something. I'm stuck in my birthday suit."

"You wait. I know Charlotte. I can't be acting all self-assured and cocky about it. It's just a matter of time."

Carl picked up some Chinese food on his way home from the studio. After eating it hungrily, he changed into a pair of loose fitting gym shorts and relaxed on his bed to memorize his lines. When the phone rang he picked it up and didn't bother to check the caller ID. "Hello?"

"Carl? Are you busy?"

"Just reading the lines. Trying to get it in my damn head."

"Want help?"

"You want to go through it?"

"I do."

"Okay. I'll try not to cheat. You start." Carl hid the face of the script.

"Okay...ready?" Carl heard him inhale, then say, "I hope it's enough for you, Troy."

"Will it ever be enough?" Carl slid down on his mattress, into the soft pillows.

"It better be. You can't expect me to keep whoring for you eternally."

"Whoring? Is that what you're doing?"

"Sex for payment? What do you call it?"

"I call it love." Carl felt a stirring in his body and it almost distracted him enough to stop paying attention.

"Love?"

Pausing, Carl struggled for a minute. Before he peeked he remembered the line. "Get over here. Now. You know I think you're incredibly handsome." Carl imagined Keith's face. "And judging by your hard-on, the feeling must be mutual."

"It's only hard because it's been a long time since I've had release."

"And I have to ask myself why." Carl reached between his

legs and touched himself. He was almost erect.

"You know why. You know what I've been dealing with. That woman is blackmailing me."

"Because?" Carl strained to listen to some movement that came across the line behind Keith's dialogue. Carl wondered what he was doing.

"Because…I've been with a man."

"Precisely," Carl said. Pausing, he added, "That's it."

"You've got it down. Or were you cheating?"

"No. I didn't look at the script. Once I get going, I'm okay. I sometimes flounder when I begin a scene."

"Carl?"

"Yes, Keith?" Carl stopped touching himself, suddenly feeling it was grossly inappropriate.

"I'm really nervous about tomorrow."

"I know. Look. When you begin to take off your clothes just look at me. Forget everyone else. I'll try my best to make you relax."

"My luck I won't sleep tonight."

"The first run through is only a camera rehearsal. So you'll get to do it without scrutiny. Next will be the dress rehearsal. Don't worry. You'll have a few run throughs before it gets serious. On the final taping, Charlotte gets a little more impatient. But by then, you'll be used to it."

"You think as this goes along, we'll get more and more scenes?"

"I do. But that's not a bad thing, Keith. On the contrary."

After a pause, Carl asked, "Do you live alone?"

"No. I share an apartment with a woman named Patty."

"Oh. Are you two…"

Carl heard Keith sigh first. "We have slept together."

"And?"

"Well, it's kind of a weird set up."

"How so?" Carl was intrigued.

"I originally moved in to be platonic roommates. But one night we just did it."

"But you didn't refer to her as your girlfriend."

"She is and she isn't."

"Does she know that?" Carl laughed.

"You know how some women get."

"I do." Carl looked down at his bare chest, wishing he had

36

someone to screw, even if it was just occasionally.

"Well, she's got this waitress job because she can't get any work acting, and she comes home completely exhausted. I don't blame her."

"But you're not getting laid."

"Exactly. And I don't want to go out and find some other woman, because if I brought a girl home it would kill Patty."

"I get it. I do."

"How about you? Are you dating anyone, Carl?"

"I was a few months ago. But it just didn't click. Now to be perfectly honest, I have decided to put my work first. I'm not actively looking."

"How old are you?"

"Thirty."

"In my book, that's still young. Besides, none of these actor relationships ever work out."

"Some do. Don't lose hope."

"Anyway, thanks for being there for me."

"No problem. Any time you need me, call."

"Thanks, Carl. I guess I'll see you tomorrow, and you'll be seeing more of me than you'd like to!"

Laughing with him, Carl shook his head. "Don't worry. Judging by what you look like in clothes, you have nothing to be embarrassed about. Strut your stuff proudly, Keith."

"You're great, you know that?"

"The feeling's mutual." Carl smiled.

"See ya later."

"Bye, Keith." Carl hung up and smiled to himself. After he set the phone in the cradle, he looked down at his cock. It was bulging from under his shorts. "What's that all about?" he asked himself. Pausing to think about whether he was attracted to Keith or not, he felt his body respond. "Oh, you have to be kidding me. This is all I need."

Chapter Four

Keith didn't get any sleep. He was tossing and turning so badly, he left Patty to sleep in the second bedroom, worried his spinning would keep her awake. By morning he was a wreck. Gulping black coffee, leaving without speaking to Patty because she was still sound asleep by the time he was ready to go, Keith drove to the studio with a knot the size of a baseball in his stomach.

Having taken extra time grooming, shaving, and preening, since he was going to be fucking naked on the set, Keith felt no matter how much deodorant he used he'd still sweat.

Seeing Carl's friendly smile, Keith hurried to meet him and get his calming words. "I'm a mess."

"You look fine. Did you sleep?"

"Maybe an hour."

"Ouch." Carl cringed. "Well, it's okay to be nervous. It keeps the edge to your performance."

"Right. Right." Keith nodded, trying to convince himself that nerves were a good thing.

Charlotte appeared next to him. She touched Keith's arm. "A word?"

Keith gave Carl an anxious glance and followed Charlotte to speak privately.

"How're you doing?"

"Nervous."

"Good. Nervous is good."

"That's what Carl said as well." Keith tried not to wring his hands.

"Look, Keith…I know this is your first nude scene."

Nodding, gulping in terror, Keith tried to pretend he was okay.

"It's all back view. No one is going to see your privates, you got that?"

"Yes. Good."

"Just go through the motions in the camera rehearsal. Don't worry too much about anything yet. Just get used to it."

"Get…" Keith leaned closer. "Get used to it?"

"You know. For the taping."

"Oh. Yes." Keith thought she meant from then on he'd be naked. What the hell was this, a porn movie?

Whispering in his ear, Charlotte said, "Betty has a little belt of something if you need it to calm your nerves."

"Do I look that bad?"

She bit her lip and nodded. "You look like you're about to be executed."

"Where's Betty?" Keith searched the set.

"Check with Marty."

"Thanks."

"See you in about ten minutes."

"Okay." Keith watched her walk away and made a beeline for Marty. "You know where Betty is?"

"Through that door."

"Thanks." Keith stood outside a wooden door. He rapped it with his knuckles. "Betty?"

"Yes?"

"It's Keith, can I come in?"

"Door's open."

Keith twisted the knob and pushed it back. Betty was sitting at a lighted mirror.

"Uh, Charlotte said you may have a shot of something to calm my nerves."

"Oh, right. The big nude scene." She reached into a drawer and removed a bottle of whiskey and a shot glass. "Here you go, darling."

"Thanks." As he poured he shook.

"Oh! My goodness. Let me help you." She took over for him.

Licking his lips, Keith waited. She handed him the glass.

"There you go, son."

Closing his eyes, Keith threw it back, choking at the potency.

"That will settle your nerves. Don't you worry, sweetheart. You're beautiful and you have nothing to be ashamed of."

"Thank you, Betty."

"Now go out there and show them what you're made of."

"I will, thanks." Leaving, continuing to choke on the burning

40

heat in his throat, Keith wondered if that was a lousy idea to have drank it and he'd be coughing through the whole scene. Heading to the refreshment table, he poured a glass of orange juice and swallowed it down to get rid of the burn. A hand on his back made him jump.

"Whoa!" Carl laughed. "Holy Christ, Keith. Calm down."

"That's easy for you to say."

"Can you do this?"

"I have to." Keith wiped his mouth.

"You don't. Just tell Charlotte you want a body double."

"Oh, shut up. Who am I, Brad Pitt?" Keith laughed at the absurdity.

Carl held Keith by his shoulders, making him look him in the eyes. "Calm down. You will do it flawlessly."

"Will I?" Keith doubted that very much.

"Just look at me. No one else."

Keith gazed into Carl's eyes. A beautiful shade of gold surrounded the green color. "Yes. I will. That does help."

"Forget the fuckers behind the scenes. It's you and me in that room. Period."

"Yes. You're right."

Charlotte's voice echoed through the studio.

"We're up, Keith. You okay?"

"I am. Just keep me focused."

"I'll do the best I can."

As he and Carl headed to the set, Keith passed Melvin. "Should I get in costume?"

"Later. After the camera rehearsal."

"Okay. Thanks." Keith kept walking. Standing in the fake bedroom, looking out at the number of employees who were going to witness his striptease act, Keith fought with his anxiety to remember to focus solely on Carl. Carl would pull him through this.

"You ready, cookie?" Charlotte asked.

"Yes."

"Right! Let's go, people!"

Carl took off his shirt and climbed into the bed. When Keith looked at him, with the blankets around his hips giving the impression Carl was nude under the covers, Keith felt chills cover his skin. Carl's torso was hairless and pure muscle. Keith was impressed and hoped he didn't look thin in comparison.

Charlotte spoke more softly, "You ready, Keith?"

"Yes." Keith wanted to come across as confident. He needed Charlotte to see he could handle the pressure.

"Okay...bedroom scene. Take one. Action!"

His eyes on Carl as he lay on the bed waiting for him, Keith began unbuttoning his shirt. "I hope it's enough for you, Troy."

"Will it ever be enough?"

"It better be. You can't expect me to keep whoring for you eternally." Keith dropped his shirt on a chair, leaning down to remove his shoes and socks.

"Whoring? Is that what you're doing?"

"Sex as payment? What do you call it?" Keith tucked his thumbs in the waistband of his jeans, tugging them down.

"I call it love," Carl whispered affectionately.

"Love?" Keith yanked off his briefs, laying them over his jeans.

Carl craned his finger at him. "Get over here. Now."

With the blankets elevated, Keith climbed into the bed with Carl.

Instantly, Carl shimmied lower on the mattress so they were at the same level.

"You know I think you're incredibly handsome," Carl purred, stroking Keith's hair back from his face. "And judging by your hard-on, the feeling must be mutual."

"It's only hard because it's been a long time since I've had release." He felt Carl wrapping his legs around him under the covers.

"And I have to ask myself why." Carl cupped the back of Keith's head.

"You know why. You know what I've been dealing with. That woman is blackmailing me."

"Because?" Carl leaned closer.

Wanting to finish the scene without screwing up, Keith tried to slow his breathing but his respirations and pulse were going wild. "Because...I've been with a man."

"Precisely," Carl replied, wriggling against him. Under his breath, Carl, hissed, "Get over here."

Keith struggled to remember if that was a scripted line. Soon everything shot out of his brain as Carl's mouth met his. It was open, but no tongue was used. As they kissed, Keith felt Carl tightening his hold around his body, drawing him to his chest.

Keith couldn't believe Carl's passion. If this was acting, it was fooling him. In reflex, Keith embraced Carl, wrapping around his neck, deepening the kiss.

Charlotte's booming roar broke their moment. "Oh, my God! Men, you have outdone yourselves. You make it look so easy." Pausing, she peeked behind her at her crew. Her cameraman gave her a thumbs-up. "Perfect. Well, if the next taping doesn't compare to this morning's we're covered."

Keith scooted back on the bed, away from contact with Carl.

Carl climbed out and slid his shirt back on.

It took a moment for Keith to recover. The scene seemed very real to him for some reason, as if there were something tangible between he and Carl. Slowly sitting up, the blanket still covering his groin, Keith realized he was hard. He had no idea why, but he was.

A woman hurried to him with a sheet acting as a blind so Keith could get dressed with some privacy, which Keith thought was absurd considering everyone had already seen him naked. Perhaps it was some protocol. He couldn't guess.

Once Keith had his jeans on, Carl approached him. "You were amazing."

"Was I? I know it sounds weird, Carl, but I can't remember if I was good or not."

"I don't know if I would have handled it as well as you did. You looked very professional."

"Thanks." Keith put his shirt on. "It means a lot coming from you. I was seriously shitting a brick. But I kept thinking of what you said, you know. Just look at you, pretend we're the only ones there."

"It worked?" Carl appeared amused.

"It must have. You said I did okay."

"I'll have to remember my own advice when it's my turn."

"Quiet on the set!"

Carl moved Keith farther from the action. "I bet they use that take. It was so fucking perfect."

"Does that mean I won't have to do it again?"

"No. You won't be that lucky. We have dress rehearsal next. Charlotte will get a couple more takes, then decide which one she likes best. Where did you get the booze?" Seeing Keith's puzzled stare, Carl said, "I tasted it."

"Oh!" Keith blushed. "Betty. Charlotte thought I needed a

little courage."

"Ah. I get it."

"How long before the next take?"

"We have to get into costume. It sounds silly considering I'm supposed to be naked and you take your clothing off but…" Carl shrugged.

Keith touched his shoulder. "Thanks again. I hope I'm not acting like an insecure pain in the ass."

"No. Nothing like that. You'll be doing it for me soon. Believe me."

Keith noticed Melvin waving at him. He acknowledged him and approached.

"Charlotte wants you to wear clothing that's easy to remove."

"Why? Did I fumble?"

"Just slightly with the buttons. This shirt has only four." He gave it to Keith.

Keith swapped tops.

"Here's that pair of black slacks that fit you so well. Just use the zipper, don't hook it."

"Thanks." Keith dropped his jeans down his legs, stepping into the slacks.

"And these loafers you can just kick off."

"I appreciate this, Mel."

"It's my job, sweetie."

At the flirtatious gaze, Keith stood straight. "I'm not gay, Melvin."

"No one said you were."

Keith continued to tuck in his shirt as Melvin led him to his make-up man.

Carl changed into a pair of gym shorts and no top. His face was powdered and his hair brushed for him. He leaned back in the chair as a light oil with tinted lotion was massaged into his chest. His vision caught Keith as he was attended to, those long, shaggy blond locks given a good brushing so they shined.

Falling into a trance as he stared at him, Carl had to force himself not to use his tongue in their kiss. It just wasn't natural to kiss someone with your mouth open and not explore it with your tongue. It took everything he had to prevent it. It went against the grain. Kissing passionately was done with a tongue. But he knew

Keith was straight and wouldn't appreciate the Frenching.

Someone jogged to where they were sitting. "It's call time. You almost ready?"

Carl nodded, waiting for his last touch of oil. Standing, he gazed at Keith who hurried over.

"Ready for round two?"

Keith laughed. "Yes. I'm much more relaxed this time. I didn't even hit Betty up for another shot of whiskey."

"Great." Carl gazed at Keith's mouth. After kissing it, he was having a hard time concentrating on much else.

Meeting Charlotte back on the set, seeing her shouting to everyone behind the scenes, Carl waited, standing next to Keith.

She spun around. "What are you doing? Get in the bed."

Carl walked around the mattress, sitting against the headboard, drawing the sheet to his hips.

"Okay! Let's get this going. The test shot was perfect so this should be a snap."

"Quiet on the set!"

Carl stared at Keith. Keith appeared so much more relaxed it was palatable. Perhaps when Carl had his first nude scene he would seek Keith's advice from now on.

As their dialogue started, Carl couldn't wait for Keith to drag those clothes off. Keith had a fantastic physique. Being blond, his pubic hair was a light golden brown, and the fur on his arms and legs was so pale you had to touch it to see it. Keith's chest and abs were ripped, pure hard muscle. His arms were sculpted and curved at the deltoids and biceps, and his thighs were long, powerful quadriceps and tight rolling calves. But the most intriguing aspect of Keith's appeal was his adorable face. The man was downright pretty. Brilliant blue eyes, that blond, perfectly groomed but shaggy mane of hair, and high cheekbones, square jaw...the list was endless. Carl couldn't believe what he looked like nude. He was astonishing. Lying in the same bed felt so damn good, Carl was angry it was acting. This man turned him on. Period. No, he didn't intend him to. He never really imagined his co-star would. How did you prevent animal attraction? You didn't. But you also didn't act on something that wasn't mutual. So you shut your mouth and pretended. Oddly though, this take, he was pretending he didn't want Keith, when the reality was the opposite.

Their lines were exchanged, that pair of silky black slacks

glided soundlessly down Keith's amazing body. Carl had to force himself to look back at Keith's eyes, knowing Keith was using his gaze to keep calm. When his briefs dropped onto the clothing pile, Carl bit his lip to stop from ogling the man's anatomy. Keith wasn't hard, but he certainly wasn't soft either.

Once Keith climbed into the bed with him, Carl wrapped his legs around him under the covers. He'd done it last time and wanted to do it again. It dragged Keith closer. He needed him closer. With only a small pair of shorts on this time, it felt more arousing, the skin of their legs brushing against each other was downright hot.

Carl stroked Keith's hair affectionately, losing himself in Keith's gaze as it connected with so much attention to his own. When their kiss drew nearer, Carl felt his skin prickle in anticipation. Moving closer, opening his mouth, Carl closed his eyes and dug through Keith's baby-soft hair, clamping his legs tightly around Keith's legs. To his astonishment a throbbing bulge pressed against his crotch.

"Cut! Perfect! Absolutely perfect. Well done, men."

Carl had to force himself to stop kissing Keith. It felt so fucking amazing.

As he returned to reality, Charlotte boasting about their chemistry and how sexy it was, Carl found Keith staring at him strangely.

Immediately Carl unraveled his legs and slid back on the bed, separating them. "You all right?"

"Yes."

Carl wasn't convinced.

A woman held out a sheet to cover Keith. Carl watched him climb out of the bed, trying to hide his erection from view.

Carl couldn't catch his breath. Holy shit. What the hell is this all about?

Moving to stand, knowing lying in the bed for too long would appear absurd, Carl got out, crossed his arms over his chest and waited for the next take.

After they had done the scene two more times, Carl walked to the dressing room quickly to change. With each repetition the comfort level between them improved dramatically. And Carl felt as if he couldn't help himself. Dragging Keith's incredible body to his, kissing him, feeling Keith's cock swell and throb against his own, Carl struggled with his feelings and knew they weren't appropriate. He felt like an idiot, and also like he needed to apologize to Keith. He just didn't know what to say he was sorry for.

Keith drove home with another new script next to him on the passenger's seat. He was trying not to think. His brain was numb. Parking, going through a robotic routine to get inside his apartment to fall apart in private, Keith closed the door behind him, tossed the script and his keys on the kitchen table, and stopped short. His eyes unfocused and blurred, his stomach churning in agony, Keith felt so humiliated he could die.

He got a fucking hard-on. Every time Carl pulled him close to his body in bed and kissed him, Keith grew erect. He was so embarrassed.

Tears burned his eyes and his throat closed up. Suddenly he was hyperventilating and having a panic attack. Sitting down on the sofa in his living room, Keith covered his face with his hands and struggled to think.

How could I do that? Carl knew I got hard! He had to feel it!

Keith couldn't face him again after that. He was mortified. "I have got to get laid! Patty! Jesus. It must be because I'm so pent up."

Knowing he had to review the next episode and get it into his head, Keith dreaded reading it.

Wiping at his nose and eyes, Keith slouched back on the cushions and struggled to compose himself. When the phone rang he flinched. Standing with an effort, he looked down at the caller ID. It was Carl.

"Oh, crap." Keith imagined letting the machine pick up, reconsidered, and felt as if he owed Carl an apology. "Hello?"

"Keith."

"Hi Carl." Keith was trying to make his voice sound carefree and light. Acting.

"Look, Keith, about what happened…"

"Nothing happened." Keith moved back to the sofa to sit down before he fell over. He knew he'd get punished for it. Knew it. Carl must be sickened by it.

"I'm sorry, Keith."

Keith thought he heard wrong. "You're sorry?"

"Yes."

"Why?"

"I don't know. I just felt as if I crossed some boundary with you. I feel terrible."

Keith tried to think and was having a rough time getting his brain to absorb the words.

"I know I was out of line. I'm sorry. I don't know what the next script has in store for us, because I'm scared to death to read it, but I promise I won't take advantage of you like that again."

"Take..." Keith was completely baffled. "Take advantage? What do you think you did?"

After a long pause, Carl whispered meekly, "Wrapping my legs around you."

Keith fought to recall him doing that and couldn't. "I don't think that was an issue." Wasn't Carl going to tell him how angry he was about Keith growing excited?

"Oh?"

"Did..." Keith stammered. "Did you do that?"

"I did. After I did it, I felt like crap. We didn't have to be tied in a knot like that under the sheets."

Keith rubbed his forehead to concentrate. "I thought you were calling to ball me out."

"What?" Carl gasped. "About what?"

"About..." Keith bit his lip.

"Keith, you were a pure professional on the set today. You remained completely composed and didn't let the fact that it was your first time doing a nude scene show. I was in awe."

"But..." Keith wondered why they were ignoring the elephant in the room. Professional? Getting a woodie on the set?

"Keith?"

Swallowing down a lump in his throat, Keith replied, "Yes?"

"If you didn't think my behavior was out of line, why do you sound so upset?"

Biting his lip, feeling like an idiot, Keith blurted out in terror, "Because my dick got hard!"

"So? So did mine."

Keith was ashamed he'd admitted it. He felt as if he couldn't face Carl after he'd said it.

"Keith, it happens. Believe me. Don't sweat it."

"Christ, Carl, I was so fucking embarrassed."

"Don't be. It's impossible to control our bodies in every circumstance. I don't know about you, but my dick has a mind of its own."

The levity finally broke through Keith's panic. "Yeah?"

"Oh, God yes."

"Like, when did it happen to you before?" Keith tried to relax his tight back muscles.

"Oh, I don't know. No, I take that back. I do. In college I offered to pose for a group of artists who got together once a week at night. I was in a pair of briefs, not nude, but I got a fucking hard-on. I have no idea why. It wasn't like I was fantasizing about sex or anything. Maybe just sitting there and being admired stimulated me."

"Could they tell?"

"Oh, hell yeah. You can't hide a hard-on behind a pair of cotton briefs, Keith."

Chuckling, feeling infinitely better, Keith let out a deep sigh. "Thanks, Carl. I swear the amount of self-flagellation I was doing was torture."

"Stop doing it. You have to forgive yourself for things like that. This business is hard enough without self-imposed pain."

Keith rose off the couch and looked down at the script for episode three. "We should look at the new copy."

"You have it there?"

"Yes. Do you want to count to three?" Keith laughed.

Carl joined him. "One, two…"

"Three." Keith opened to the first page.

"Here we go."

"Where? What page are you on?" Keith held the phone between his cheek and shoulder, using two hands to flip through the manuscript.

"Page five. Top."

Keith folded it back, read it, and smiled. "At least we're not naked."

"No. Not at that kissing scene. Let me flip through it."

As he heard Carl moving on the other end of the line, Keith read the notes in detail. It made him smile. He and Carl were supposedly coming back from dinner out, soaked from rain, and teasing each other sexually. It was an outdoor shot. Another first.

"Aha."

"What?"

"My fucking turn."

"Oh, no way." Keith wanted to burst out laughing.

"Last scene. Check it out."

Keith hurriedly flipped pages. Pausing, he read the directions. "About time!"

"I am so fucking petrified."

Keith sat down at the kitchen table with the script at his elbow. "Don't be."

"At least you didn't get a hard-on until you were in bed. What do you want to bet I get one even before I take off my fucking pants."

Keith felt so much warmth fill him at Carl's candidness it was amazing. "You'll be okay."

"Ha!"

"Just pretend it's just me in the room. I got that advice from a great guy I know." Keith shoved his tongue into his cheek.

"That guy was lying."

Keith broke up with laughter.

"You sound better now."

"I am. Thank you so much, Carl. I swear, I'd be so lost without you."

"Ditto. I really feel lucky you were cast in that role. It could have gotten ugly if it wasn't someone so sweet."

Feeling his cheeks blush at being called sweet, Keith became bashful.

"Let me let you eat and relax. We get enough of this show all day."

"Right. I'm glad you called, Carl."

"Me too. See you in the morning."

"See ya." Keith hung up, sighing with relief.

Carl's smile faded as he walked away from the phone. Sitting on the couch, script in hand, he read it more carefully so he could fully grasp what was expected of him. It appeared Dennis and Troy's budding relationship was the lead story. The amount of lines he had had doubled from last season. The affair was supposed to change from one of strained obligation to carefree courtship. There were several shots filmed outdoors as well. He and Keith outside a restaurant, drenched from rain, kissing and spinning in glee. He moved the script aside for a moment to think.

Carl reclined, resting his head on the back of the couch. Closing his eyes, he envisioned the episode with perfect clarity, and couldn't wait to film it.

Chapter Five

The street had been barricaded off for filming. Keith stood calmly as he was attended to by Ken. His shine buffed off with a powder puff, his hair tousled to perfection.

"Kind of pointless to preen, Ken. I'll be soaking wet in a minute."

"Oh, well. We have to go through the motions."

"How the hell do they fake a rainstorm when it's so sunny out?"

"You're asking me?" Ken pressed his fingers to his chest. "Probably some kind of dimmer switch in the camera. Who knows? I'm just surprised everyone on television isn't some avatar computer graphic."

That made Keith laugh.

"Nice dimples!" Ken pushed his index finger into one.

Keith swatted his hand away playfully. "Behave."

"Why? I think you're gorgeous. Don't tell me to behave."

"I'm not gay, Ken."

"So? Think it matters to me? I still get to touch you."

Keith smiled, flattered. How strange. A comment like that would have enraged him only a couple of weeks ago. Now? It didn't do much to bring out a reaction in him either way.

Someone leaned against his back.

Looking over his shoulder, Keith found Carl's cheeky smile. "Yes?"

"Seems ridiculous to get made up and then soaked."

Keith pointed to Carl with his thumb, addressing Ken, "See?"

"Oh, shut up, you two." Ken waved to shoo them off. "Telling everyone how to do their job."

Chuckling softly, Keith turned around and found Carl's big smile. "You look dashing in your suit."

Carl reached to adjust Keith's tie. "You do as well. May I?"

"Thank you, sir." Keith nodded in gratitude.

Charlotte's roar alerted them.

"Show time." Carl nudged Keith.

They headed over to the front of the restaurant. Keith noticed a water truck was spraying down the pavement.

"Right. How are my boys? Ready for some fun?"

"Yes, ma'am." Keith grinned at her.

"Good. Okay, go inside, and come out when I cue you."

Carl opened the door to the restaurant and they both stood behind the glass waiting.

"Do it right or we'll be changing in and out of clothes all morning."

"Me?" Keith laughed. "You're the one with your lines written on your palm."

Carl hid his hand, giving Keith an impish grin.

Water suddenly came pouring down in a rain shower.

Behind him, Carl was singing It Never Rains in California under his breath.

"You're going to make me go into a laughing fit."

"Sorry." Carl jumped. "Oh, that's our cue."

They stepped out of the front door, looking up at the rain.

"Shit!" Keith shouted. "Should we get a cab?"

"No, let's run for it!" Carl replied.

"No, let's get a cab. We'll be soaked!"

"We're already soaked!" Carl hugged Keith, spinning him around.

"You're insane!" Keith laughed, the drops running down his face.

After a meaningful pause, where Carl gazed into Keith's eyes, they kissed.

Keith wrapped his arms around Carl neck as they rocked side to side, the rain pelting them while extras ran in and out of the scene with umbrellas.

The kiss was so intense, Keith had to plant his tongue on the bottom of his mouth not to use it.

As they mashed lips, Keith peeked under his eyelids to see Carl's expression. It was on fire.

Parting, smiling at each other, Carl grabbed Keith's hand and shouted, "Let's go!"

Breaking up with laughter, Keith gripped his hand tightly and they ran down the street.

"Cut!"

The water shut off and assistants raced to them with towels.

Keith took a small hand towel and wiped off his face, rubbing it over his head.

Someone else helped them remove their soaked jackets.

"Well?" Carl asked as they walked back to Charlotte who was watching it again on the monitor.

"What can I say?" Charlotte smiled in pleasure. "The two of you are burning up the screen."

"Are we?" Keith asked in surprise.

She beckoned him over.

Still using the towel to dab at his neck and hair, Keith gazed at the television monitor.

The scene played back.

As he absorbed it, Keith could almost feel the real attraction growing between their two characters.

"Well?" Charlotte asked impishly.

"Yeah. Looks good."

"Good?" she scoffed.

"No. Great." Keith turned to ask Carl, "What does she want me to say?"

"It's wonderful!" he shouted in exaggeration. "Charlotte, the show will win an Emmy!"

"All right," Charlotte scolded. "Go change and head back to the studio for the next scene."

As Carl walked to a trailer, Keith joined him. "You ball buster."

"Someone's got to keep her in line." Carl opened the door and they entered, continuing to get out of their wet clothing and into replacements for the next scene.

Keith kept his back to Carl, giving him privacy. He knew what was coming, Carl's turn to flash his bottom to the world.

Once he was clothed, Keith spun around. Carl was tucking in his shirt, zipping his fly.

"Right. Shall we?" Carl gestured to the door.

Keith exited the trailer and approached a waiting car. They climbed into the back seat.

"You ready?" Keith asked.

"Hell no." Carl's legs spread in a wide straddle as he slouched.

"You'll do fine."

With his gaze out the window, a slight curl edged up the corner of Carl's mouth. "Yeah. Fine."

Wanting to comfort him, Keith squeezed Carl's knee.

Instantly Carl's eyes darted to the contact.

"Don't worry."

Carl rested his hand over Keith's and held it. "I'm trying not to. Thanks."

The car parked outside their studio. After they climbed out, standing in the sunshine, Carl suggested, "They may be a while. Want to get some coffee?"

Keith turned to where he was pointing. They entered a cafeteria, dim by comparison to the outdoor light, and filled two paper cups with hot coffee.

After sitting down together, Keith sipped it, making a face at the taste.

Carl laughed softly.

Abandoning the cup of terrible coffee, Keith ran his hands through his damp hair. "I'm calling my parents this week."

Carl perked up, giving Keith his attention.

"The show airs the beginning of the month. I have to tell them."

"I was contacted by my agent to do an appearance on Ellen."

"No shit?"

"No shit." Carl sipped his coffee.

"Well, I suppose it's good publicity."

"When are you going to do some?"

"I don't know. I haven't thought about it. I figure my agent will call me."

"You'll have a few spots before and after it airs. I remember most of the cast members did something to promote it. Bet someone asks me if I'm gay."

Keith winced. "I'm dreading that."

"Don't let it bother you. Inevitably, every handsome actor gets the label sooner or later."

"I hate to admit it, but I always think men who play gay guys in the movies and television are either queer or bi."

Carl started laughing.

"I know. Well, I'm older and wiser now."

"I suppose the label doesn't bother me."

"No?" Keith asked in surprise.

"No. It keeps people interested. And I don't mind being the

object of a gay man's desires. It's flattering."

"Really?" Keith wondered if he felt the same.

"How insulting can it be? Come on, Keith. People form attractions. Big deal. And in this career?" Carl made a face as if to say it was widespread.

"Well, most of the assistants are either women or gay men." Keith took a quick scan around the room as they spoke.

"And they're out. They don't hide who they are. You have to give them credit for that."

"If you were gay, would you come out?"

Carl set his empty paper cup aside. "That's a hard fucking question."

"Is it? With me it's a no brainer."

"No?" Carl smiled.

"No. I'd never come out in public. I hear after you do that, the straight roles dry up. You can't play a leading man in a romantic film."

After Carl checked his watch, he looked back at Keith.

Keith wondered if he was still thinking about a retort, or he had nothing to add to the subject. "I'm not just saying that. I mean, I've read it in the tabloids."

Carl leaned across the table towards him. "It's just about living a lie and being paranoid about people finding out, and outting you, or living like you would like to and being open."

"I suppose. But at least we don't have to worry about it."

"No." Carl rose up. "We better head back to the set."

Keith picked up their coffee cups to toss out on their way to the exit. Once he opened the door to the bright sunlight, he gazed back at Carl. He appeared very deep inside himself.

Keith wondered if he was beginning to get nervous about the next scene.

When they were walking across the lot to their studio, Keith put his arm around Carl's waist. "You'll do fine. Don't worry."

Carl wrapped his arm around Keith as well. "Now you're the expert at being naked?"

"No. Hardly. I just want to give you the confidence and support you've given me."

"Thank you, Keith." Carl squeezed him tight.

"My pleasure."

"I will get a woodie."

"I know." Keith giggled wickedly.

Carl stopped at the restroom before they had the next taping. After he relieved himself he washed his hands and found his reflection in the mirror. Sighing deeply, trying to psych himself up for what was coming, Carl rehashed Keith's comments over coffee. There was no doubt he was becoming attracted to his handsome co-star. There was also no doubt his adorable co-star was not attracted to him. End of story.

The erection he was dreading was not about nerves. It was about sexual desire. The number of times he and Keith had kissed, touched each other lovingly, hugged, it was as if he was already in a relationship with him.

But he wasn't. It was an emotional vacuum. All it was was acting. Pretending. It ain't an act anymore, sweetie.

Carl dried his hands and left the bathroom. Seeing everyone gathering on the set, waiting for him, he hurried his pace, his nerves becoming shot.

Keith watched him as he approached. Carl felt so much heat wash over his body at the sight of him, he was in agony suddenly. Looking away from his stare, Carl tuned into Charlottes instructions.

"...back from the restaurant and hot to trot. You come through the door, shedding your clothes as you go, kissing..."

Carl peeked at Keith. His attention was on their director.

"Any questions?" She paused. "Good. Let's go."

Carl's assistant wet his hair down with a pump bottle, the damp jacket was given back to him to slip on. Carl closed his eyes as his face was sprinkled with water drops.

He walked behind the backdrop set and stood still.

"You okay?" Keith whispered, touching Carl's hand.

Carl's heart was going berserk in his chest. "Yes. Shh. Let me focus."

Keith retracted his hand.

"Bedroom scene, take one! Action!"

Counting to three in his head, Carl pushed through the front door into the living room. He spun around and caught Keith as he jumped on him, kissing his lips. Once they parted mouths, Keith began pushing the jacket off Carl's shoulders. It dropped by their feet.

"I adore you!" Keith moaned, kissing Carl's neck, sending

58

chills washing over Carl's body.

"Oh, Dennis. I had no idea it could be like this."

"Neither did I. All I want to do is get you naked all the time."

Carl was hyperventilating, struggling to keep his composure as Keith unraveled his necktie and dropped it on the floor with his jacket.

"Get me naked," Carl choked out, though he was becoming an emotional wreck. As he paused, holding onto Keith's upper arms, Keith had his shirt unbuttoned and tugged at it to remove it. Carl released his hold on Keith, the shirt fell soundlessly.

As Carl watched, fighting to stop gasping for air, Keith knelt down and unbuckled his belt.

A moan of agony was threatening to hiss out of Carl's throat. Keith had his zipper open and was urging Carl's trousers to fall around his ankles. Stepping out of them, kicking off his shoes and yanking off his socks, Carl was down to just his briefs in seconds.

Keith gazed up at him, still kneeling. "Troy, you are so incredible."

Swallowing for courage, Carl waited, his back to the camera, as Keith pressed his fingers into the top of his briefs and they began moving down his thighs. He was so fricken hard he was going to die. Closing his eyes, praying he'd think of anything but the gorgeous god who was about to pretend to give him a blowjob, Carl was about to pass out.

Holding Keith's shoulders for balance, since he was about to fall over from the fear, Carl forced himself to continue, stepping out of his briefs as Keith held them to the floor. Biting his tongue to stop the scream welling inside him, Carl glanced down. Keith smoothed his hands over his hips, his ass, while staring at his erect cock.

"You're magnificent," Keith crooned.

In between beating himself up, Carl had to remember his lines. "I adore you." It came out like a sob.

Keith's gaze darted to his at that moment. Carl had no idea what he was betraying on his expression. Acting! Please! I'm acting!

Keith leaned closer, as if taking him in his mouth.

Finally, Charlotte yelled, "Cut!"

"Oh, God," Carl cried, covering his erection with both hands.

Keith immediately held Carl's jacket in front of him. An assistant rushed to hold up a blind. As he was cut off from the rest, Carl shivered in spasms of terror as he stepped back into his clothing. He didn't even want to look at Keith.

While he was closing his zipper, he heard Charlotte shout, "Perfect!"

"Thank fuck." Carl didn't think he could do it again. Once he had a shirt on, he rushed off of the set to compose himself.

Keith was stunned. He felt so miserable for Carl, he wanted to cry. Seeing him rush away, Keith made a move to go after him, pausing to think if it was the right decision.

Leaning over the sink in the men's room, splashing his face, Carl's emotional sob choked out of him before he bit it back. Finally forcing himself to regroup and calm down, he noticed Keith poke his head into the room.

"You okay?"

"That was the hardest fucking thing I have ever had to do in my life."

Keith approached, reaching out his arms.

Carl embraced him, battling the urge to weep again. Gulping down his feelings like a bitter pill, Carl stepped back from Keith and wiped at his eyes. "I'm such a fucking wimp."

"Oh, no way. You know how much guts it takes to do that? You are not a wimp, Carl. Not by any standard."

"I was very close to having a breakdown and not finishing the scene."

"I could tell."

"Christ."

"I think to everyone else it came off as passion. Don't worry. After all, it met with Charlotte's approval."

"Why is she doing this to us?" Carl moaned.

"Ratings?"

"It's fucking with my head, Keith."

"How so?"

Another man entered the men's room. Carl gestured for them to leave. But he didn't want to answer Keith's question. How could he tell him the pretend attraction was beginning to feel all too real?

As they returned to the set, Keith rubbed Carl's back in

comfort. It only tormented him more. Carl knew it was a platonic touch. It always would be.

Charlotte noticed Carl's expression the moment he returned. She held his hand and drew him away from everyone else, including Keith. Once they were standing in a private corner, Charlotte said, "Shit. What's going on?"

"Nothing. It was just a tough scene."

"Did you and Keith have a disagreement?"

"No. Nothing like that. Are you kidding me? I couldn't have done it without his support."

A knowing smile curled the corners of her lips.

He shook his head in admonishment. "No. We're not."

"I'm not saying a word." She threw up her hands innocently.

"I know you. You'd like nothing better than to see your two main stars in a real romance. It would boost your ratings through the roof."

"Maybe. But the two of you have the most amazing chemistry, Carl. The heat blows us away when you touch. The camera is lapping it up, believe me."

Carl rubbed his face in frustration.

"What? Tell me. I can't have you going cuckoo on me in the first three episodes of the new season."

A sob cracked his words. "I do like him. Okay?"

"Did he reject you?"

"No. I don't want him to know. He's completely straight, Charlotte. Please, don't tell him."

"Oh, sweetie." She hugged him. "It's endearing. And it'll make the passion between you sizzle."

"My God!" Carl pushed back, laughing in amazement. "Ratings! Ratings!"

"Sorry. You know I love you. I love all my characters." She pecked his cheek. "So? You'll survive the next episode?"

As she began to make her escape, Carl asked, "What on earth do you have us doing next time?"

A twinkle in her eye as she left, Carl felt his skin cover with chills.

Changed back into his casual clothes, the new episode script in his hand, Keith waited for Carl to do the same. Leaning against the wall by the exit door, Keith found him approaching and stood.

"Hey."

"Hey."

"You…ah, you want to grab dinner somewhere?"

"Sure."

"We could read the new script together." Keith opened the door to the bright outdoor light.

"That's fine, Keith."

"You look really beat. You want to take a rain check?"

"No. I'm fine. How do you want to work this? You want me to drive?"

"I can follow you. Where do you want to eat?"

"I don't care. You decide."

Seeing Carl fingering his keys and looking anywhere but directly at him, Keith felt uncomfortable. "You want to just call for a pizza and eat it at my place?"

Instantly Carl met his eyes.

The power of his stare made Keith's breath catch in his throat. Carl had the most intense green eyes he'd ever seen on a man.

"Yes. All right." Carl pointed to his car. "I'm parked over there."

"Okay. I'll meet you." Keith waved as he walked to his car. The look on Carl's face puzzled him. The poor guy was probably still trying to get over the shock of the nude scene. He could relate.

Pulling in front of that sleek black Corvette, Keith imagined earning enough money to trade in his five-year-old Subaru. Wouldn't that be nice?

Checking his rear view mirror as he drove, Keith kept getting distracted by his thoughts. Kneeling in front of Carl while he was naked, and the size of his damn erection. The guy was so hard during the scene, Keith felt humiliated for him. Though Carl's back was to the camera and crew, Keith knew someone else must have seen it. It was so fricken big.

Stopping at a traffic light, Keith felt his body respond ever so slightly to the memory of the scent of cologne or spicy men's soap that had drifted towards him from Carl's nude body. Inhaling deeply, combing his fingers through his hair, Keith had to admit to himself he thought Carl was attractive. Well, the guy was amazing. And seeing him vulnerable like that, knowing he was dying inside, it turned Keith on to the point of embarrassment.

That was a harsh reality Keith was not prepared to accept. This was just the result of not having any sex. He was convinced if he and Patty were going at like bunnies every night, he'd have no interest whatsoever in anyone else.

But he wasn't. So, seeing Carl's flawless physique naked and excited was making him horny.

"You're not queer," he told himself, wondering why he had to. "You are acting. That's all."

His eyes darting to the rear view mirror, Keith's cock tingled.

Carl was a good friend. Nothing more.

Carl parked in a guest space at Keith's apartment complex. He could tell by the look of the place it was for those with a modest income. He'd lived in his share of low income flats and was hoping those days were gone forever.

Meeting Keith in the lobby, both with the script in their hands, he waited as Keith opened the door, climbing the stairs behind him, gazing at Keith's ass as he went.

Once they were inside the apartment, Keith set his keys and the paperwork on the kitchen table. "What do you like on your pizza?"

Placing his copy of the script down as well, Carl leaned on the counter as Keith thumbed through the yellow pages.

"I don't know. Anything."

Keith met his eye. "Are you okay?"

"Drained."

"I hear ya." Keith picked up the phone. "Hello? Yes, I'd like to order a pizza for delivery."

Carl left him alone and walked to the living room inspecting the worn furniture and below average details. Sitting down, he kicked off his shoes and relaxed on the sofa, staring at Keith while he finished the call.

"Right. Thirty minutes," Keith advised when he hung up.

"Okay."

Keith brought both copies of the script with him, sitting next to Carl. "Here."

"Thanks. Are you going to call your folks?"

Keith cringed. "I should. I just can't get up the nerve."

Carl smiled sadly. "Welcome to my world."

"At least they already know you're working on a cable TV

drama."

"Why do you think your parents would be so upset?"

"I'm probably overreacting."

"I'm sure you are." Carl wanted to touch him, but didn't.

"Okay, what on earth does Charlotte have us doing next episode?" Keith opened the first page of the manuscript.

Carl lost himself on Keith's profile, admiring him silently.

"She's got us kissing again."

"Damn her." Carl laughed.

"Hey...this is new."

"What?" Carl leaned on his shoulder, wanting to connect to him.

"We have a spat. Look. It says you slap me."

"Do I? And? Next page make-up sex?"

"She didn't wait 'til the next page."

"Oh?" Carl snuggled against Keith so he could read it with him.

"Look. It says I say something that pisses you off, you slap me, and when I go to nail you, we end up sucking face on the floor."

"Nice."

Keith met his eye. "Funny."

"Sounds hot."

"I suppose it is. You think people really get off on watching us kiss?"

"I do." Carl sat back as Keith turned to face him.

"Gay guys?"

"Possibly. And women."

"Women?"

"Yes. You don't think two men touching gets some women off?"

"Really? Women?"

"I'm not joking." Carl opened his script to read the details.

"That's hilarious. I never imagined that. I'll have to ask Patty when she gets home."

Just remembering "Patty", Carl asked casually, "What time does she get in?"

"After ten."

"Oh." Carl nodded, it was just nearing six.

"You want to try to learn some lines?"

"There's not a lot of dialogue, thank fuck."

"No," Keith laughed with sarcasm, "it's all sex!"

"I think Charlotte has lost her head."

"Maybe she's one of those women who get turned on by two men."

Seeing Keith's sexy smile lit Carl up instantly. "Most likely." He imagined putting his arm around Keith, urging him to his chest, kissing him, with tongues. Unfortunately for Carl, he knew in reality the punch would come to his face. Not some playacting swipe and recoil.

"She's a perv."

"Either that or she's a brilliant writer and director."

Nodding in agreement, Keith replied, "Yes, you're right. She always writes and directs a major hit series."

"Exactly. She's giving them what they want."

"Whoever them is. Hey, you want a beer?"

"Sure." As Keith walked to the kitchen, Carl gazed at him sadly. You can't always get what you want. Right? "Right."

Carl lay in bed. It was nearing midnight and he had just jerked off thinking about kissing Keith. Recuperating, the spatter of his come on his chest, Carl's yearning to turn Dennis and Troy's love affair into a reality was beginning to wear him down. He didn't know how long he could stand it. Episode after episode? Kissing, stripping naked with him? What about next season? Would they still be at it?

The first episode was set to air. Little spoilers were beginning to pop up in advertisements. His talk show taping was this weekend. The cable website had a synopsis of the upcoming debut. Photos of the cast members papered the site.

Releasing his hold on his cock, Carl climbed out of bed to the bathroom to wash up. Standing at the sink, wiping his body with a wet washcloth, Carl felt slightly pathetic to be pleasuring himself over Keith's kiss. Like he was some crazed fan who hankered after the unattainable stars.

Shutting off the bathroom light, he crawled back into bed, curling into a ball, wishing for something that would never come true.

Chapter Six

Keith was dressed in his character's clothing, made up, and going over his lines in his head.

Again, Keith had been rebuffed by Patty as he attempted to have sex with her. Throwing up his hands in frustration, Keith left her to sleep on his own. Rolling around on the spare bed with so much sexual tension pent up he was about to go to a bar and find a drunk, willing partner. Instead, he jerked off. Something he had not done since he and Patty became intimate. He was afraid to do it while lying next to her in the bed at night, fearing she'd think he was a nasty pervert. But alone, in that second bedroom, he had to. He was dying for release.

After he'd come, he felt his cheeks burn at his thoughts. The direction they had taken to help him along didn't include Patty.

Seeing Carl being preened for their coming scene, Keith's skin covered in chills. Images of Carl stripped naked, his cock blushing with color because it was so hard, Keith swallowed with an uncomfortable gulp.

When someone touched his arm, he jumped in shock.

"You okay, sweetie?"

"Yes. Sorry." Keith grabbed his chest to stop his pounding heart.

Charlotte looked to where Keith had been gazing. Keith felt his skin go bright red at being caught admiring his delectable co-star.

"Uh huh." She seemed to be digesting it. "Anyway, you ready for your big fight slash make-up scene?"

"Yes."

"I knew you would be." She kissed his cheek.

As she walked away she began shouting for everyone to get in place. Keith waited for Carl.

"Hey."

"Hey."

Keith felt shy suddenly, knowing he'd jerked off to thoughts of this man. "You ready?"

"As I can be."

"Don't whack me too hard."

"Promise." Carl winked.

They took their places. Keith was concentrating on his character, imagining the lines and actions in his head. They'd already had a dry run. This was for a live taping.

"Fight scene. Take one. Action!"

Instantly transformed into their roles, Keith felt Carl shove him into the room. "What the hell do you think you're doing?"

Keith confronted him. "You don't fucking own me!"

"Don't I?" Carl puffed up, menacing.

"You think just because of this trial, I have to pretend I'm your slave?"

"No. You don't pretend. You are my slave!"

"Screw you!" Keith braced himself.

Carl slapped him, open handed, and quite hard. "Shut up! Don't you ever talk to me that way!"

Getting over the power, Keith held his stinging cheek. "You bastard." As he went to return the favor, Carl gripped his wrist. They struggled until Carl threw him to the ground.

It was rougher than the rehearsal, a hell of a lot rougher. Keith was trying to stay in character and not moan in pain. Carl had him pinned with his body weight. And the fact that he was much more muscular and taller, Keith was trapped by his size and determination.

Carl released his wrists and grabbed his face, urging it to his lips. Something happened. Keith didn't know what. But this wasn't like the other kisses.

Carl was devouring him.

"Baby, I'm sorry. I never should have hit you. Forgive me. Forgive me," Carl sobbed.

Keith wrapped around him, rolling over so he was on top. He gripped Carl's jaw in both hands and sucked on his face, whimpering at the passion. His tongue slipped into Carl's mouth. Keith hadn't intended it to, but it was painful planting it and holding it still in his own. Carl seemed to go wild under him. Soon Carl's tongue was inside his mouth and Keith completely lost track of what they were supposed to do next.

Finally Charlotte shouted, "Cut!"

Keith jerked back, still sitting on Carl's hips. "What?" he panted, unable to catch his breath. "Did we fuck up?"

"No sweetie. You're done with that scene."

Keith felt like dying. Everyone was staring at him. And there were so many fucking people in the room. A hand touched his arm. Wrenching his gaze away from the gawking crowd, Keith gasped for air and found Carl smiling up at him.

"Can you let me up?"

"Oh!" Keith stumbled to his feet. "Sorry!" He held onto the wall to steady himself.

"Did I smack you too hard?"

"Huh?" Keith was in a daze. His head was spinning. "No. Let me go for a sec. I have to take a minute to regroup."

"Keith?"

As he walked away, Keith touched his mouth. His skin felt raw from Carl's rough shadow. His cock was throbbing in his slacks. Staggering into the men's lounge, Keith shut himself into a stall and leaned his back against the closed door.

Rubbing his face, dragging his fingers through his hair, Keith felt as if the walls were caving in on him and he couldn't breathe.

"I'm insane. I can't be feeling this. What the hell's going on?"

But he did. He did feel it. Carl was so sweet, so genuine, so caring. That man was making this transition into acting so much easier for him. The guy was a saint. Patiently guiding him, nurturing him, and...

Keith was so petrified of the physical attraction, he was nauseous. Imagining retching, throwing up in the toilet, Keith felt his skin become dewy with perspiration.

"Keith?"

Carl's voice. It was deep, masculine, and he adored it.

"Keith? Is that you in the stall? Are you all right?"

Swallowing down some black water from his nerves, Keith inhaled deeply, opening the door.

"Oh, Keith. You look pale." Carl hurried to him. "I never should have hit you so hard. Christ, I am so sorry."

"No. I'm okay."

Carl brought him to the sink, dampening a paper towel and mopping Keith's brow. "Forgive me. I was just afraid if I lightly slapped you, she'd make us do it over. I know her. She needs the scenes to be real."

"I'm sorry." Keith nudged Carl's hand aside, stopping him from wiping his face.

"Sorry? For what?"

"When…" Keith choked up. "When I kissed you…"

"Oh, that. Believe me, it's okay. It's hell keeping your damn tongue still, isn't it?"

Almost crying with relief, Keith accepted Carl's embrace. As Carl rocked him, he whispered, "Don't upset yourself over this nonsense."

"I felt like I violated you."

A soft laugh emerged from Carl. "No. Not in the least."

"It's just the moment was so intense."

"Yes, it was. It's what makes Charlotte wet herself."

Keith laughed. It broke his nervous anxiety instantly. Pulling back to gaze at Carl, Keith said, "What would I do without you?"

Carl stroked Keith's cheek gently. "I left a red mark. I'm sick about it."

"It's okay. I can't even feel it anymore."

"You ready for our next scene?" Carl stood back, holding Keith's hands.

"Yes. Let me just wash my face."

"All right."

Keith stood over the sink, seeing Carl's reflection behind him. It felt so good to have Carl there with him it made his chest swell with warmth.

Carl led Keith back to the set. He knew everyone was watching and wished they'd lay off the poor man.

"You ready, snookims?" Charlotte baby-talked to him.

"I am." Keith smiled bravely.

"Ken!" Charlotte hollered. "Make up the poor boy."

Carl stood by as Ken powdered Keith and brushed his hair, adding a nice blushing reddish tone to the cheek that had been slapped.

Once Keith was tended, Carl looked back at Charlotte.

"Okay, here we go. Live taping…get into position."

Moving to his place in the room, Carl opened his zipper and untucked his shirt.

"Make-up scene. Take one. Action!"

Stuffing the shirttail back into his slacks, Carl zipped his pants, fastening the top button. "I love make-up sex."

Keith buttoned his shirt and cuffs. "You love any kind of sex with me."

Meeting him on his side of the room, Carl wrapped his arms around Keith's waist, pressing his pelvis into his, rocking him gently. "It's because I love you."

Keith's eyes seemed to well up with emotion. Carl was constantly amazed by his talent and professionalism.

"Oh, Troy," Keith sobbed, hugging him tight.

Carl stroked his hair, kissing his head softly. "We were meant to be together, Dennis. I don't think we can fight fate."

"I never meant for this to happen."

Smiling sadly, Carl tightened his hold on Keith, loving the heat and scent of him. "Me neither, Dennis. But you can't deny it. Love just sometimes happens."

Hearing Keith sob, Carl almost broke the scene, unsure if this was acting or not. Holding out, not reacting to it, Carl paused as Keith's eyes connected to his. Tears were running down his cheeks. It alarmed Carl and he knew it wasn't scripted.

"I'm so happy we found each other," Keith managed to get out before he hiccupped with his sob.

Carl wanted so much to ask him if he was okay. This was very odd. "Me too, lover. Me too."

When they kissed, Carl felt his toes curl at the affection. Either Keith was the best actor on the planet, or Keith was falling for him and couldn't prevent his emotions. Whatever it was, it was mesmerizing.

"Cut!"

Slow applause began to ring out. Carl leaned back to see Keith's face. "Are you all right?"

"Yes." As Keith smiled, more tears ran down his cheeks.

Carl was not convinced.

Charlotte rushed over. "Oh! I love it! Keith, you are brilliant. The raw emotion is so fucking perfect for your character. Augh! Someone restrain me before I marry him!"

Laughing as he wiped at his eyes, Keith kept meeting Carl's gaze shyly.

"Okay, boys and girls, same time tomorrow. We'll finish up the episode and I'll get you the new script. Well done!" Charlotte patted both of their backs.

Pinching Keith's chin between her thumb and index finger, Charlotte whispered, "You are amazing."

"Thanks."

"Go home. Relax."

As she vanished, Carl kept his eyes on Keith.

"Come on, let's change and get out of here." Keith walked to their wardrobe area.

Taking off his shirt, handing it to Melvin, Carl was worried about Keith. Once they were in their street clothes, Carl walked Keith out of the studio building.

Before they parted ways, Carl stopped him. "Is the pressure getting to you?"

"Huh?" Keith appeared confused.

"Keith, crying wasn't scripted. You didn't do it in any of the rehearsals."

Keith shrugged weakly. "Felt right."

"It felt real." Carl touched Keith's cheek. The one he had slapped.

"Good. That's very flattering." Keith laughed softly. Then, as if seeing Carl was not laughing with him, he added, "Look, it was the intensity. Don't read more into it. The slap was harder than I anticipated and it brought out more emotion. Depth. It must have been okay because Charlotte really seemed to like it."

"Are you sure that's all it is?"

"Yes. I'm fine. See you in the morning."

"See ya." Carl watched as he walked away. Keith wasn't fooling him. There was more to that passionate play than Keith was willing to admit. And Carl knew why.

Looking over his shoulder, seeing Carl staring after him, Keith gave him a small wave and sat behind the steering wheel of his car. "Shit." He started the engine, and felt the lump return to his throat. He fucking loved the guy. Okay? So? Sue me! Leaving the parking lot, wiping at his eyes as they once again filled, Keith bit back a sob of frustration. How the hell could you spend every day, kissing, touching, speaking words of love to someone, and feel dead, nothing. Acting? Oh yeah, he was acting. Keep telling yourself that, Keith.

"Oh, Christ, Carl..." Keith dabbed at his eyes. "Why did you have to be so fucking amazing?"

Managing to maintain some self-control as he drove home, Keith came through his door and dropped his keys on the table. The light was blinking on his answering machine. He moved across the room to it and hit the play button.

"Keith? It's Mom. I just wanted to touch base with you. Any luck with auditioning? Call and catch me and your dad up. Love you."

Sitting down on the couch, composing himself, he picked up the phone and dialed. He'd put it off long enough. The damn premiere of the show was coming up.

"Dad?"

"Keith! Sandy, Keith's on the phone!"

Keith waited until his mother picked up an extension.

"Keith?"

"Hi, Mom."

"You weren't home when I called. Were you just out or did you get a job?"

"I got a job."

His dad asked, "In acting?"

"Yes."

His mother cheered in excitement. "Tell us all about it!"

"You know that new cable series called, Forever Young?"

"Yes! Oh, Ron, you know that one, with Betty Blue, Omar Desmond, and Carl Bronson."

"Oh! Yes. Right. Well done, Keith!"

"Is it a decent size part, Keith?" his mother asked.

"It is. I'm actually quite an important character in the new season."

She squealed in excitement again so loudly, Keith had to pull the phone away from his ear.

"Oh, God! Tell me about it! Keith, I am so proud of you. You see? Patience paid off."

His father added, "And him finally getting Adam Lewis as his agent helped."

"Oh, I am so thrilled!"

"What's the character you play?" his father asked.

"Well, I can't tell you too much, you know, it's all kept secret for the premiere."

"We're your parents! You can tell us," his mother shouted.

"The character's name is Dennis Jason."

"Xavier's brother?" his mom gasped.

73

"Wow, you are a fan." Keith shook his head in amazement. "Yes, Xavier's brother. I play a guy who's being blackmailed and needs Troy to get him off the hook."

"Oh, isn't Carl Bronson adorable?" his mother gushed. "I swear he's my new heartthrob."

"Sandy, he's half your age," Ron scolded.

"Oh, hush. He is not. Keith. I am thrilled. We need to take you out to dinner to celebrate. Do you want to ask Patty and we'll take you someplace nice?"

"Uh, sure. But not yet. I'm really busy with the rehearsal schedule."

"Oh, of course...well, we need to make a plan. Ron, tell him we'd like to take him out someplace nice."

"He's on the line, he can hear you, Sandy. Keith, just give us a ring back when you can make it. No rush."

"Okay, Dad."

"Honey, I have never been so proud of you."

"Thanks, Mom. See ya, Dad." Keith said goodbye, hanging up. "You wouldn't be so proud if you knew I had a hard-on for your 'heartthrob'." Keith spread out on the couch and stared at the ceiling, trying not to get too depressed about his life. After all, he was going to be a star.

Sighing, Keith closed his eyes and rested.

Carl heated up some leftovers in the microwave. His gaze kept being drawn to the telephone. He wanted to hear Keith's voice. The bell sounded for his food. He opened the door and set the plate on the table. Taking a bite, Carl kept losing himself on the amazing kiss, Keith entering his mouth with his tongue. Carl sat in silence, the fork hovering over his plate, his food going cold. He wanted it to be for real, not make believe. And if Keith did feel something for him, how on earth was he going to convince Keith it was okay?

Chapter Seven

After his morning shower, Keith dressed in a pair of jeans and a cotton shirt. Behind him, Patty was sleeping on the bed. He hadn't waited up for her last night. Instead, he slept in the spare bedroom and was asleep by the time she came home. As he filled his pockets with his wallet and keys, she opened her eyes, giving him a groggy stare.

"Hey."

"Hey," she echoed, stretching to see the time on their clock radio. "Are you going to sleep in the other room from now on or something?"

"I don't know. I just don't want to bother you."

"Is something wrong?"

"You tell me." Keith paused, knowing he had to get going.

"It's just… It's…"

"What?" Keith implored.

"Never mind." She burrowed back into the pillows.

"Patty, eventually we need to talk about this."

"I know."

"I have to go. When are you off?"

"Monday."

"Great." He shook his head in frustration at having to wait all weekend.

She rolled over so she could see him again. "I called my agent."

"And?"

"Nothing. Not a fucking thing."

"I'm sorry, Patty. I did talk to Adam. I tried."

"I know. I'm not blaming you."

"Just hang in there."

"Whatever."

He bent down to peck her cheek. "See ya later."

"See ya."

As he walked to his car in the lot, Keith was beginning to understand why Patty had become distant. Jealously. He knew how he'd feel if she was offered a lucrative position in a number one drama. He'd be gutted. This was not helping a friendship which was already strained. And thinking of moving out? Having her pay all the rent? It sounded infinitely cruel. He just couldn't do that to her.

The car was hot from the morning sun beating down on it. Keith opened the windows and turned the radio louder. As he drove to the studio he was pumped to see Carl, wondering what sexual contact they were in for next.

Carl kept looking behind him, checking for Keith's arrival. He had the latest script for episode four and wanted to chat with him about it. Sitting in a folding chair, absorbed in the titillating new love scenes he and Keith were going to be performing, Carl felt hands on his shoulders from behind. Looking at one, he instantly recognized Keith's fingers and trimmed nails. "Hello, hot stuff."

Keith cuddled him from behind on the pretext of reading over his shoulder. "Uh oh. That's the new one."

Feeling Keith's cheek against his lit Carl up instantly. The urge to kiss him, run his lips over the stubble of his jaw was overwhelming.

"More perversion."

"Oh?"

The scent of Keith's aftershave, his shampoo, his skin, was driving Carl absolutely insane. "Yes, look here." Carl wanted him to keep snuggling, so he pointed to a paragraph on the script that was resting on his lap. "It says we're at a dinner party with my parents at their home. No one knows we're a couple. You, naughty boy, you lure me out onto an outdoor patio to kiss me. And, my oh my, we're exposed as being homosexual."

Keith rested his chin on Carl's shoulder. "Bummer."

"It was bound to happen." Carl wanted to purr and nestle his cheek against him. It was hell holding back.

"So, Dennis and Troy are outed. Do we get shunned? Placed in a leper colony?"

"No. At least not yet." Carl flipped a page. "It says my

mother slaps me for embarrassing her. I wonder how Betty's right hook is."

Feeling Keith pull away, Carl was sad when he moved a chair over and sat down. He liked being cuddled.

"Good. Your turn to get clobbered." Keith leaned over to gaze upside down at the script.

"Are you still upset about that?"

"No. I'm joking." Keith met his eyes, giving him a smile.

Carl wanted to lick at his dimples desperately.

"I told my parents I was in the show."

Closing the script on his lap, Carl gave Keith his undivided attention. "And?"

"I left out the gory details. I just said I got a part on Forever Young. Turns out you're my mom's newest heartthrob."

"That's really sweet." Carl needed to touch him.

"So…" Keith stretched his back, his arms reaching over his head. "At least they know I'm working."

"They have to be pleased with that, Keith. They know what the competition is like." Carl savored the glimpse of Keith's lower abdomen when his shirt gapped from his jeans.

After his cat-like stretch, Keith rested his elbows on his knees so he was closer to Carl. "They are. With the information they have at the moment, they are."

"Good enough."

"Uh…"

"Yes?" Carl mirrored Keith's position, so they were nose to nose.

"I…I think Patty's jealous."

Sitting back with a start, Carl gasped, "Of us?"

"No!" Keith narrowed his eyes at him. "Of the fact that I got an acting job. Us?"

Carl wished he had a rock to crawl under. "That's what I meant. Us. The fact that we're working." God, shoot me.

The suspicion in Keith's sky blue eyes was doing two things to Carl. One, turning him into putty because he was so damn sexy, and two, scaring him.

Someone was shouting at them. It was time for a read through of the new script.

As they rose up off the chairs, Carl fell in behind Keith as he walked off, admiring his ass and legs. Cool it, Carl, just fucking cool it or this good working relationship will end.

Keith had to force himself to focus on the lines he was speaking. Since they were doing nothing more than a speed reading, Keith was left to imagine the scenes in his head. The next kiss on the patio had two words written in italics near the dialogue, as if it were emphasizing the action, "very passionate". A very passionate kiss. What the hell had they been doing up 'til then? Keith assumed each kiss they shared had to have that ingredient. Hadn't they been kissing up to Charlotte's standards?

When they took a break for some coffee and the restroom, Keith decided on finding out exactly what he and Carl's smooching had been lacking.

"Charlotte?" Keith whispered softly as she filled a cup with black coffee.

"Yes, sweetie pie?"

He held the script in front of her and pointed to the words as he said, "Very passionate."

"Yes."

"Like in we haven't been kissing passionately up to now?"

A light, jovial chuckle preceded her answer. "No. That's not what I mean."

"Then, more of the same?"

"Uh. No." She had a quick look around first before she added, "It's really obvious you guys aren't kissing like...uh, like..."

"Like? Like?" Keith waited in anticipation.

"I take that back. You had one."

"One?" Keith was completely lost.

"How do I say this tactfully?" She tapped her smile with her index finger.

He got it. "French kissing."

"Yes." She pointed at him as if he'd answered the million dollar question. "I'm sorry, Keith. But you can tell the difference. On those scenes we come so close to your faces we can see every detail."

Keith felt his skin break out in chills remembering the one kiss he and Carl exchanged that was completely intoxicating. He began to pant thinking about it.

Charlotte cupped his face, forcing him to meet her eyes. "You okay?"

"Yes. Just digesting it."

"Jesus, Keith, don't hyperventilate."

He was humiliated it was that obvious he was.

"Forget it." She waved her hand. "Do what you're comfortable with. We'll manage." She walked away.

Keith could feel her disappointment spinning in her wake.

His hands on his hips, the script still in his right one, Keith stared at the floor trying to regain his composure.

"Keith?"

Carl's warm hand glided to the back of his neck. Keith's skin ignited at the sensuous touch.

"You okay, babe?" Carl lowered his head to connect with Keith's stare.

"Yes." Keith tried to snap out of his mood. When Keith stood straight, Carl's hand slid off of him. "I...I was just confirming something in the notes of the script."

"Can I ask?"

Sighing deeply, Keith pointed to the words. "This. Very passionate."

"And? What did she say?"

"She says on the close ups of us sucking face that she can tell we're not using our tongues."

"Really?"

"Yes."

"And that bothers her?"

"So it seems."

"We did French kiss once." Carl's gaze was so intense it was making Keith weak at the knees.

"I know. So, no big deal right?"

Carl shrugged. "I suppose not."

"You...are you okay with it?"

"Come here."

When Carl cupped his face and kissed him, pushing his tongue into his mouth, Keith dropped the script and wrapped around his neck. Their mouths open and their tongues going crazy swirling around each other, Keith's cock was so hard he was in agony.

As Carl parted from his lips, Charlotte's voice whispered from right next to them, "See? That wasn't so hard, was it?"

Keith jumped back, wiping his mouth with the back of his hand nervously.

She winked at Carl and walked off.

"Did she ask you to do that?" Keith couldn't stop his heart from exploding in his chest.

"No. I just figured I'd give us a rehearsal. No big deal, right?"

Was he kidding? Seeing Carl's calm confidence, Keith shook his head slowly. "No. No big deal."

"Problem solved." Carl walked over to the refreshment table and picked up a bottle of water.

Once he did, Keith kept touching his lips, as if the sparks of electricity lingered. No, Carl. Problem far from solved. The problem keeps getting worse.

On the way home Keith stopped off at the diner where Patty worked. Sitting at the counter, he tried to get her attention as she rushed back and forth from the kitchen to the tables.

He read the menu and waited for her to notice him.

"Keith?"

"Hey."

"You here to order food? Or for me?"

"Both."

She took out her pad. "Shoot."

"I'll take the cheeseburger and curly fries. And a cola."

"Okay."

"You have a minute?"

"Let me put your order in and check. I'll be right back."

He set the menu in the stand and watched her continue to race around. A few minutes later she set his soda down with a straw.

"How was rehearsal?"

"Good. My parents want to take us all out for a celebration meal."

"When did you call them?"

"Yesterday."

"Did you tell them it was a gay part?"

Cringing, Keith looked around the area to see if anyone heard. "Please be quiet about that."

"Sorry."

Keith didn't think she looked sorry in the least. "Patty, it's me that should be apologizing."

"Why?"

"I feel badly that I finally got work and…" he gestured to the diner.

"That's life. Let me see if your burger is done."

Sipping his cola through the straw, Keith felt very guilty. He just didn't know what to do about it. He couldn't find her work. Only her agent could.

She emerged from a double door with his order. "I have to get going again. Can we talk more at home?"

"I try but you're usually not receptive to it."

"I'm just worn out."

"I know."

She left him sitting there, staring after her. This wasn't good.

Carl stopped at a bar on the way home. It was Friday night and he didn't want to hide in his condo just yet. Sitting at the counter, he ordered a beer and checked to see if his mobile phone was on. He considered calling one of his drinking buddies, reconsidered, and stuffed the phone back into his pocket.

The bartender returned with his order. "Aren't you Carl Bronson from Forever Young?"

Blushing at being recognized, which didn't happen very often, Carl nodded. "Yes."

"I love that show! Isn't the new season beginning next month?"

"Yes. It is."

"Can I have your autograph, man?"

"Sure." Carl waited as the bartender found a pen and paper. "You want me to write just my name? Or?"

"No. Write 'to Dave' on it."

Seeing the man's name tag with the same name, Carl wrote, To Dave, I'm flattered you like the show, all the best, Carl Bronson. After he finished he handed it to him. "Is this okay?"

"Yes. Perfect. Thanks."

Carl went to give him some cash for his drink.

"No. On the house."

"That's very generous of you."

The man nodded and left to help another customer.

Smiling warmly, Carl knew the show was still in its infancy, and he wasn't exactly swarming with paparazzi. But it felt nice. Being noticed, acknowledged. And he had his taping of the talk show this weekend. More publicity, more air time…it had to be a good thing.

Leaning his elbows on the bar, relaxing as he sipped his beer, Carl used the opportunity of a pause in his thoughts to remember Keith's kiss. Charlotte wanted them to use their tongues? Oh, that is so fantastic. Yes, it was missing. Carl had a feeling you could tell. And the damn strain of holding back when all you wanted to do was enter…

Inhaling, Carl felt his body go rigid. A stream of air hissed from between his teeth he was so excited. He flipped out his phone, wanting to call Keith, hear his voice.

Pausing before he finished dialing, he shut it down and pocketed it again. No. Don't harass the man on his time off the set.

Blurring his vision on the rows of liquor bottles behind the bar, Carl went back to his fantasy. He wanted another bed scene. Something really crazy. One where they were both naked and exploring each other's bodies while kissing. He wondered if he could ask Charlotte to add a scene like that. After all, they wanted racy passion. The straight characters were all over each other already. His and Keith's scenes seemed restrained by comparison.

Imagining them both nude, touching, caused Carl to moan out loud.

Blinking, coming out of his dream, he finished his beer and headed home, in need of sexual release.

Keith went through the same routine once he got home, tossing his keys and the new script on the table, kicking off his shoes. He began peeling his shirt over his head, imagining lying in bed with the script and dozing off after reading through it.

Stripped to his briefs, he brushed his teeth and washed up, grabbing the script as he walked to the spare bedroom.

Turning on a light, he propped himself up on the pillows and began memorizing.

Very passionate.

Carl's tongue entering his mouth. "Oh, Christ…" Keith moaned. Reaching into his briefs, feeling his erection, Keith set the script aside and began jerking off. Visions of Carl's naked body, his engorged cock, that kiss. Keith closed his eyes and increased the speed of his hand. Arching his back as he came, feeling the come spatter his chest, when the phone rang he was startled. "Shit." He jumped out of bed and grabbed toilet tissue from the bathroom, stumbling to the bedroom to pick up the extension. "Hello?"

"Hey. Bad time?"

Hearing Carl's sexy voice, Keith instantly blushed in embarrassment at having jerked off to thoughts of his co-star yet again. "Uh…"

"You want to call me back?"

"No. It's okay." Keith sat down on the bed, flipping his dick back into his briefs.

"What were you doing?"

His cheeks burning with shame, Keith cleared his throat. "Just reading the script."

"Me too. Christ, it's so hot it's making me crazy."

Keith blinked in confusion. Was Carl having the same reaction to it as he was? "Yeah?"

"Jesus, Keith, pretty soon it'll be x-rated."

Keith laughed in reply, scooting back to sit up against the pillows so he could reach the script he'd set aside. "No. She can't do that on cable."

"Oh? Then you don't remember the Ties That Bind very well, do you?"

Keith took a moment to try. A vague recollection of side shots of nudity as a young couple experimented with sadomasochism sprung to his mind. "No. She wouldn't do that, would she?"

Carl gave out a sarcastic laugh. "If it's after eleven at night? Oh yes, she can."

"I suppose we'll cross that bridge when we get to it. I remember last season only Cheryl and Omar had sex scenes."

"That's right. And they were very steamy and controversial. The publicity Charlotte got from them screwing on camera was amazing."

"I do remember that!" Keith recalled the big hoopla over the event. "She had some religious right wing group of mothers picketing somewhere."

"Yup."

"Christ, she's tempting fate doing it with a gay couple."

"No she's not. She's hoping for it. Are you kidding me? That's free advertising."

Smiling at the thought, Keith teased, "What can she do that she hasn't done? I've already supposedly made love to you and sucked you off."

"Accent on the word supposedly."

Excited at the potential of them doing things together, Keith just laughed it off. "Shut up. She can't do that."

"No. Perhaps you're right."

"You sound disappointed." Were they flirting?

"Oh, I am. Crushed."

Keith's cock throbbed. "So, uh, you have that talk show taping this weekend." He touched himself lightly.

"I do."

"Are you nervous?"

"No. Not at all. Those are a piece of cake. I'm not taking off my clothing."

Keith chuckled, fixing his penis to lay upright as it grew hard again.

"So how far have you read into the new script?"

"Just the beginning. Up to our 'very passionate' kiss on the patio. Why? What else is there?"

"I've skimmed it, you know, looking for the good parts."

Good parts? Keith pumped his cock a few times in excitement. "And?"

"Well, after the evening disaster you're comforting me."

"Am I?" Keith's hand moved in a steady rhythm.

"Yes."

"What am I doing?"

"Don't you have the script with you?"

Looking down at it while both his hands were occupied at the moment, Keith asked, "Can't you just tell me?"

A pause followed. Then a very cagy comment of, "What are you doing that you can't flip through the script?"

Keith took his hand away from his dick. "Nothing."

"Are you being naughty?"

The sexy tone of Carl's voice made the hairs rise on the back of Keith's neck. What? Did he have a secret camera on him?

"Are you touching yourself, Keith?"

Completely shocked at being caught and speechless, Keith wanted to hang up on him and crawl under the covers. Finally finding his tongue he laughed nervously, "No! Come on."

"No? I am."

The wash of excitement that spread over Keith's body was intense. "Shut up. Stop kidding."

"Anyway…if you have a free hand…" Carl continued, "Look at page fifteen, bottom."

Sitting up and opening the script, Keith flipped pages to the correct one. "Uh oh."

"Oh yes. She's at it again."

"It looks like we're just shirtless." Keith kept reading.

"Only in the beginning. We get down to our briefs together. But, get this, you lick me."

"Lick you?"

"Yes. What part are you up to?"

"The part where we're sitting…ohhh," Keith found it. "I'm licking your chest."

"You are. We take off each other's clothing."

Growl! Keith used his thumb to wipe the shimmering drop from the tip of his cock. "Huh."

"Huh?"

"Well, what do you want me to say?" Keith pumped his dick a few more times, milking out the pre-come.

"I don't know. I suppose you can deal with it. After all, you pretended to give me a BJ."

Keith closed his eyes and shivered at the words. It was like phone sex.

"Keith?"

"What?"

"What are you doing? Tell me the truth."

Yeah right. "Nothing. Why do you think I'm doing something?"

"It just sounds like you are."

"So, what else does she have us do after I lick you?"

Another pause followed, then in a very sensual, deep voice, Carl whispered, "You lick my chest, all over. Then you lap your way to my mouth, and we suck on each other's tongues."

Keith closed his eyes and fisted his cock with more determination.

"Then, after we kiss, very passionately, you push me back on the bed and rub your hands all over me, grinding your hips into mine."

Keith inhaled a sharp breath and came, the strength of the climax made his skin shiver and his semen hit him under the jaw.

"You naughty, naughty man…" Carl purred.

"I…I have to go…" Keith tried to speak normally.

"Uh huh."

"So, see you Monday?"

"You will, you sexy mother fucker."

"Right. Bye. Oh, good luck with the taping."

"Uh huh."

"See ya." Keith hung up, knowing Carl knew what he had done. He felt like an idiot, but he couldn't help it. And Carl was egging him on with all that dirty talk.

Looking down at the second mess he had to deal with tonight, Keith sighed tiredly and knew he was going completely insane to have done that over the phone. He just couldn't help himself. Carl's voice was so fucking sensual, and he couldn't resist touching himself.

"Oh, I am so fucked. How on earth can I be attracted to him? Augh!"

Carl was stunned. After he set the phone back in its cradle, he lay in bed staring at the wall for a few minutes imagining Keith jerking off at the other end. "Son of a bitch! You are attracted to me." Carl dug his hands into his briefs and massaged himself. He had already masturbated before the call, and now wanted more. He should have done it the same time as Keith, but he was so shocked Keith was doing it, he couldn't believe what he was hearing. So? Did they declare their love for one another? Or what?

Chapter Eight

All day Saturday Keith studied the script to memorize his part. When Patty finally rolled out of bed at around noon, he sat with her at the kitchen table for a much needed conversation. He couldn't wait until Monday. That was absurd.

As she munched toast and sipped sweet, milky coffee, Keith stared at her tired expression sadly.

"Are you content with our relationship, Patty?"

"What relationship? You're not even sleeping in the bed with me anymore."

Keith didn't want to cause her anymore grief than she was already dealing with. But he didn't want to cheat either.

"When I first moved here," her brown eyes riveted to his, "I didn't think we'd ever cross the line from a friendship to a relationship."

"And? So?"

"Well, I suppose deep in my gut, I knew it was a mistake and that we should have probably kept our lives separate."

"Gee, thanks."

"Patty," Keith sighed. "Do you really think we're suited for each other? Be honest."

She shrugged, eating her last bite of toast. "I figured once you got an acting job you'd break it off with me and move out."

"Ouch! Jesus. You make me sound like a monster."

"Are you?" Her eyes narrowed at him.

"I haven't even gotten my first paycheck yet." The guilt crept into his gut. He had no idea she would make his life complicated. But he only had himself to blame. He slept with her against his better judgment. Watching her avoid eye contact and sip her coffee, he asked sheepishly, "So, you think this relationship is worth pursuing?"

"Not if you don't."

When she stood to set her cup in the sink, he felt the cold shoulder. "I don't know what the right thing is to do, Patty."

"If you move out, at least give me some notice so I can put an ad in the paper."

It made him feel sick to his stomach. Her casual attitude and supposition that the minute he found suitable work he'd leave her, stung. He hadn't felt as if he had that "malice aforethought" mentality. Things just happened.

She left the kitchen without a backwards glance. If she loved him, needed him, wanted him to stay, why didn't she say that?

He knew why. She didn't love him.

Slumped in the chair, staring at the flooring through his straddled legs, Keith didn't love her either. He never had. He really appreciated her, liked her, and thought she was a decent person, but he never felt those strong emotions for her. And that's why having sex with her was unforgivable.

Carl walked off the set of the chat show with the live audience, feeling relieved it was over. Checking his phone for messages, he listened to a few from friends and was waiting to hear one from Keith. He hadn't called. Closing it and dropping it into his pocket, Carl left the studio and sat in his car. The producers had allowed him to drop the bomb that he was going to be involved in a homosexual relationship in the new season. Charlotte wanted it out as a teaser. A benign clip was shown for the television and live audience of he and Keith in their first scene together, one where they talked but didn't touch. Watching the action on the screen, he and Keith in character, Carl was amused at the way they appeared and the natural chemistry between them. They couldn't hide the fact that they liked each other. He knew the signs of two co-stars at odds. It was like nails on a blackboard to view. Painfully forced. That was the opposite of what he and Keith looked like.

They looked like lovers for fuck's sake.

"Soon the rumors will abound, babe. And you will have to deal with it no matter what you feel inside." Carl turned the key and started the engine. "Oh, fuck it." He took his phone out again and dialed Keith's.

"Hey!"

"Hi!" Carl loved his voice. It sent shivers all over him.

"Are you at the taping?"

"Just finished."

"How did it go? Did they skewer you?"

"God no. Nothing like that. It was a cakewalk, I've told you. I like doing these promotions. They're fun."

"Where are you?"

"In the studio lot."

"Oh?"

"Where are you?" Carl couldn't help but sound seductive. He was crazy about this man.

"At the mall."

"Shopping?"

"Killing time."

Carl checked the clock on his dashboard. "Can we meet for lunch?"

"Sure!"

"Which mall?"

"Lakewood Center."

"Oh? If I remember right they don't have a very good selection of decent chow. Just chain and fast food."

"I'm open to suggestions."

"You know the Original Fish Company on Los Alamitos Boulevard?"

"I can find it."

"I'll meet you in their parking lot."

"Cool. Wait for me. It might take a while. I have to walk back to my car."

"Okay. See ya there." Carl shut the phone down and couldn't wipe the smile off his face. "I adore you...I simply fucking adore you..." he sung happily.

Slowing down when he read the sign for the restaurant, Keith pulled off the main road and noticed Carl standing near his car in the lot. He parked as close as he could to him, slipping his keys into his pocket as he hopped out.

Seeing Carl decked out in silky pair of designer slacks, a back crew neck shirt with a black blazer on top, Keith licked his lips in excitement. The man had so much style and class, Keith wondered if that came with experience or was bred.

"You're looking stunning, Mr. Bronson."

Carl appeared very surprised at the compliment. "Why thank you, sir."

"I assume you had the ladies swooning in the audience."

Carl smiled sweetly at him as they approached the main entrance. "They do shriek a lot on that show. Gives me a headache." As they approached the host, Carl said, "Table for two."

"This way, gentlemen."

Keith grew hungry, sniffing the air and checking out the plates on other diners' tables.

They sat down, took the menus, and thanked the man.

"Anything to drink?"

"I'd love some ice water. I'm parched." Carl checked with Keith.

"Water will be fine." Keith didn't feel like drinking alcohol at one in the afternoon either.

"Very good."

Once the man left, Keith stared at Carl as he read the menu. The amount Keith had been thinking about Carl since he last saw him on Friday was bordering on obsessive. Jerking off while he talked on the phone with him? Unbelievable. Why had he done that?

Why? Look at him!

When Carl's long, dark eyelashes raised up and his green eyes met Keith's, Keith felt his insides twist. Instantly he lowered his head to read the menu.

"The clam chowder is awesome here," Carl whispered, moving his leg to contact Keith's under the table.

Keith's cock went rigid against his thigh in his jeans. "Is it?"

"I highly recommend it."

"I'll get that and a salad."

"Perfect." Carl set his menu on top of Keith's. Leaning his elbows on the table, Carl clasped his hands together and stared at Keith from over them.

Keith waited for Carl to say something. His gaze was hypnotic. They didn't speak. Keith became lost on Carl's handsome features.

The waiter set two bottles of water on the table, distracting them from their dreams. Keith moved back.

"Are you ready to order?"

Carl said, "Yes. Two bowls of clam chowder and two side

salads."

They both requested the same salad dressing, ranch. Once the waiter left, taking the menus, Carl resumed his position with his elbows on the table and asked, "Where were we? Oh, yes." He continued to stare at Keith without speaking.

Keith grew nervous. "So," he tried to break the strange staring contest, "tell me what the interview was like."

Carl twisted the top off the water bottle and poured it into the glass provided. "Good. I told you. A cakewalk."

"Did they ask you anything about our characters' relationship?"

"Yes. The producers wanted me to let the world know."

As Carl sipped from his glass, Keith watched him, almost losing track of his thoughts. "Did they?"

"Of course."

"And? What did you say about it?"

Placing the glass down in front of him, licking his lip, Carl replied, "That I'm madly in love with my co-star."

Keith caught his impish smile and laughed. "You're trouble."

"I am."

"I mean, did they get nosy? Push you about the gay thing?"

"No. Of course not. You know that show. The host is gay. Don't be silly. It was done very tastefully. All the support you could wish for."

"Good. That's really cool." Keith felt his mouth go dry from an unsettling nervousness that was creeping up on him. The sensation of Carl's knee rubbing against his, his rigid dick, and his desire to jump over the table and French kiss his co-star was making him dizzy. He opened his own bottle of water and drank from the neck.

Carl appeared as enrapt as Keith had been.

Keith rested the bottle on the table and toyed with the cap.

"So," Carl cleared his throat, "have you memorized all your new lines?"

"Pretty much."

"You're such a show off."

Smiling at his tease, Keith nudged Carl's leg with his.

"Are you flirting with me?" Carl asked sensually.

Feeling his face go crimson, Keith tried to cover his growing attraction. "Just getting into character. Trying to rehearse."

"Oh? Is that a fact?" Carl appeared enchanted with the idea.

"So, whenever I get the urge to be Troy Wright I can just swoop down on you for a kiss? Just to practice?"

Keith was burning up. He knew, being fair-complected, he couldn't hide his blushing cheeks and by now he was convinced the rosy color was running down his neck. "No. I was joking." *Oh, God, help me. I am so fucking excited I need to come!*

"Too bad. I thought it sounded like fun." Carl sipped his water again.

They went back to the staring game. Keith knew he couldn't get enough of it, but had no idea why Carl was playing this way. *Was Carl as attracted to him as he was to Carl? Was that sane? Hell no!*

"What's taking the food so long?" Keith tugged at his collar. "Is it hot in here?"

Carl couldn't hide his hilarity. Breaking up with laughter, he shook his head adoringly. "Christ, Keith," Carl dabbed at his eyes as they teared up. "You are too fantastic for words."

"Am I?" Keith felt the contagious laughter and started giggling.

"Yes." Carl kept busting up with it, having a terrible time stopping.

Soon they were both laughing in a riot, for no reason, holding their stomachs and trying to stop. People began staring at them.

When Keith controlled himself somewhat, he reached for his bottle of water. Carl trapped his hand around the top.

The smile fell from Keith's face and his eyes widened as they met Carl's serious expression. Catching someone spying it, Keith withdrew his hand quickly. "Don't do that."

Before Carl could respond, the waiter arrived with their soup. Carl smiled up at the man. "Thank you."

"Aren't you Carl Bronson from Forever Young?"

Before he admitted it, Carl smiled at Keith. "Yes. I am."

"I'm a big fan of that series. I can't wait for the new episodes."

"I'm very glad. Thank you."

"Can I have your autograph? It's for my girlfriend."

"Of course."

Carl reached for the man's pen, signing a piece of paper. Keith hoped one day soon, someone would recognize him, and he could be signing his name for a fan.

"Thanks. I appreciate it. I'll get your salads now."

"No problem."

Feeling slightly melancholy from his own aspirations not quite attained at the moment, Keith dazed off as Carl began sipping his soup from his spoon.

"It's fantastic. Try it." Carl ripped a slice of sourdough bread off the small loaf in front of them.

"That must feel really cool."

"It does." Carl smiled. "And by next month, you'll be doing the same."

"I doubt it."

"Why? You're loaded with talent, Keith. You're as beautiful as a pin-up boy and you're sweeter than honey. Why on earth shouldn't people line up to meet you?"

Lifting his spoon and stirring the thick soup, Keith imagined that being possible.

"Stop beating yourself up again."

Keith met Carl's scolding eyes.

"Eat."

Tasting the soup, Keith moaned, "Mm. It's excellent."

"I thought you'd like it." Carl smiled wryly at him.

"Thanks, Carl."

"Don't mention it."

After the small but satisfying meal, Carl walked with Keith out into the sunshine. "Okay, good lookin', time for me to go home and memorize."

Keith walked to Carl's 'Vette and admired it. "Nice car."

"You like? It was extravagant, but I didn't go outrageous with the condo, so I had to do something."

"I love them."

Carl dangled the keys at him.

"You're such a tease."

Choking at the comment, Carl replied, "Look who's fucking talking!"

"Me?"

"Shut up and get in." Carl stuffed the key into Keith's palm.

Walking to the passenger side, Carl watched as Keith opened the door and crawled into the low slung driver's seat. Reclining next to him, Carl purred, "Nice, huh?"

"Oh, yes." Keith fondled the leather interior.

"Take it for a spin."

"Your car? No. I couldn't."

"Why the hell not?"

"Do you have time?"

Carl rolled his eyes and fastened his seatbelt.

The minute Keith ignited the engine he moaned. It was so sexual it sent tingles down Carl's body.

Wanting to grab hold of Keith's thigh in his tight jeans, Carl sat on his hands so he wouldn't molest the man.

Keith backed out of the space and met the roadway. "Ah! I have to buy one. I am so excited."

Peering into Keith's lap, he muttered, "I can tell."

Allowing Keith to drive around, keeping quiet and savoring sitting with him, wanting to touch him very much, but restraining his urges, Carl relaxed and imagined them a couple. A real, committed couple. The amount he wanted that surprised him.

After fifteen minutes Keith returned to the lot, idling the engine while they parked near his Subaru. "Thanks. That was a real thrill, Carl."

"Any time."

Before Carl opened the passenger door, Keith gripped Carl's hand. Whipping his head around to see him, Carl found painful longing in Keith's expression. "Keith. Stop torturing yourself."

"It's what I do best." Keith's lip started trembling.

"Oh, sweetie, don't."

"I'll see ya Monday."

Before Carl could respond, Keith had exited his car and was sitting in the Subaru. Climbing out of the passenger's seat, Carl waved to him as he drove by, leaving the parking lot. Dropping back down behind the wheel, Carl growled in frustration and put the car in gear, heading home.

Keith battled with blurry eyes the entire drive home. Wiping them roughly, holding back his emotions, he parked in the lot and hurried to get inside the privacy of his home. When he came through the door, Patty was there.

He wasn't prepared for that.

Turning away from her eye contact, he closed himself into the bathroom and leaned over the sink to compose himself.

"Keith?"

"Yeah?"

"You okay?"

"Yeah. Just had to piss." He lifted the lid and urinated in the bowl. "I thought you'd be at work."

"I was. Had the early shift."

"Oh." He flushed, running the water in the sink to wash his hands and face. When he found his eyes in the mirror, he wasn't happy with what he saw. Knowing he couldn't stay in the bathroom all afternoon, he did the best he could to hide his tears and stepped out.

"What happened?"

"Nothing. Allergies." He passed by her to sit on the sofa in the living room.

"Allergies?"

"Look, just drop it." He picked the script up off the table and reread the lines he already knew by heart.

"Fine." She left the room, closing herself into the bedroom. A minute later he heard the television. Throwing the script down again, Keith stared out of the window, wondering what the fuck he was going to do.

Chapter Nine

"You ready for 'very passionate' kissing?" Carl taunted as Ken brushed Keith's hair.

"Yes…" Keith answered slowly, watching Ken pause and continue as he eavesdropped.

When Ken signaled he was finished, Keith nudged Carl to walk away from him. "You did that as a tease. The poor man is gay, Carl."

"Poor man? Just because he's gay he's a poor man? Shut up. For a man who's kissed another man, you do say some stupid things."

"I haven't kissed you for real."

"Oh? Is there a difference?" Carl perked up.

"Yes. This is acting!"

"Oh," Carl humored him.

Charlotte's commanding voice boomed over the noise. The entire cast had been assembled for the party scene. Several quick shots of conversations with other cast members were going to take place before the discovery of them French kissing on the patio.

Keith crossed his arms over his chest as he watched his fellow actors perform. He loved it. They were all top-notch in his book and he had learned something from each one. They had so much experience he was in awe of them.

He and Carl did a quick scene, exchanging a few lines with Betty who played Carl's mother. Soon it was their chance to up the passion once again.

A patio with a string of soft lights illuminated the set. It was a pretty backdrop and Keith was amazed at how authentic the fake homes were. No detail was spared.

"Get over here, gorgeous."

Keith blinked at Carl's sensual expression and tone. His skin lit up and he hadn't even touched him yet. "Moi?"

"Shut up and come closer."

"Yes?" Keith grinned, staring at Carl's mouth soon to be connected to his own.

"Don't get all weepy on me."

"Oh, shut the fuck up." Keith laughed.

"You're a mushball. I know your type."

"I am not a mushball. How insulting!" Keith loved the banter. Loved it.

"You ready, boys?" Charlotte roared.

"Yes, Mother!" Carl quipped. "She wants us to really suck face, cutie pie."

"I know what she wants. She wants slutty porn."

"Exactly."

"Then we'll give her slutty porn."

As if it were spoken like a dare, Carl wrapped his arm around Keith's waist and tugged him close, connecting their cocks. "You tell 'em, tiger."

"Ready when you are!" Keith waved to Charlotte playfully as he and Carl stood apart.

"Don't you just love them?" Charlotte gushed.

"Patio scene. Take one. Action!"

Carl purred in a low deep voice that sent the chills coursing over Keith's body, "You know how hard it is to pretend I don't want my hands all over you?"

"Very hard." Keith rubbed his palm over Carl's crotch, totally unscripted. Pausing, seeing if he had flustered Carl, Keith waited.

"You drive me insane."

Carl's cock went stiff under Keith's hand. "We shouldn't. Someone will see us."

"Screw it. Think I care what my mother and her stuck up friends think?" In response to the tease, Carl grabbed Keith's crotch.

Stifling a choking gasp from the surprise grope, he read the mischief in Carl's eyes. "Obviously not." Keith forced the lines to come out steady and not with a choking laugh.

"Obviously not," Carl crooned, stroking Keith so wonderfully, Keith wanted to kiss him. He didn't care if it was the next action in the script or not. Cupping the back of Carl's head, Keith opened his mouth and closed his eyes.

Carl connected to him with so much intensity Keith imagined

98

light bulbs bursting around them. Keith immediately used his tongue. Suddenly the two of them were licking at each other's mouth and lips, sucking hard and lapping like mongrels. Keith groaned in pleasure as Carl's hand stroked him to new heights. "Oh, God…" Keith whimpered, again, unscripted.

"Troy! How could you!"

Knowing that meant they had to stop, Keith had to physically tear himself away from this man's mouth. Completely spaced out from the tantalizing contact, Keith felt Carl move away and answer Troy's mother's accusations.

"I love this man! I don't give a shit who knows."

Betty pointed to Keith in horror. "You love him? What are you saying?"

Keith kept feeling waves of passion rushing over his body and screamed at himself silently to behave and pay attention.

"Yes! Okay?" Carl roared, "I'm gay! Now you know. So? Disown me? Beat me? What? I don't care. You won't separate us."

Betty let fly her slap at Carl's face.

It seemed hard and Keith cringed for him. Immediately after the strike, Keith was gripped again in a powerful arm. Carl had connected him to his side. Keith knew he had a line coming and was struggling to decide when.

As the pause grew and Carl nudged him, Keith looked at him curiously.

"Cut!"

"Shit." Keith knew he'd fucked up. "Right! I remember. Sorry."

Carl smiled at him smugly. "Gotcha."

"Shut up." Keith laughed.

Charlotte approached him with the script in her hand. "Your line is, 'We're not gay. He's just my lawyer.'"

"I know. I just blanked out." Keith tucked in his shirt tails nervously.

"Okay. Let's go. I want it in one take. Back to the beginning." She walked away, shouting at the cameramen and lighting crew to get ready.

Carl hissed, "I knew I'd frazzle you. Groping my cock? Two can play that game."

"Shit. I feel so stupid. And Betty has to slap you again. Ouch."

"Don't worry. It was hardly a slap in my book." Carl whispered, "Do you regret having to do it again?"

"No." Seeing Carl's demonic smile, Keith added, "But not because of that."

"No...of course not."

"Stop patronizing me, asshole." Keith shoved him playfully.

"From the beginning!" Charlotte ordered.

Keith felt Carl's arm around his waist again. Oh, hell who was he kidding? He could do this all day.

"Patio scene! Take two! Action!"

Carl looked even wilder as he repeated the first line. He didn't even wait for Keith to react before he reached down between his legs and stroked his cock. "You know how hard it is to pretend I don't want my hands all over you?"

"Very hard." Keith struggled with a coming laughing fit and Carl instantly knew it.

"You drive me insane."

"We shouldn't. Someone will see us." Keith was about to swoon from the heavy petting. That hand knew just how to touch him. He pressed his hips forward, harder into Carl's palm, trying not to hump it.

"Screw it. Think I care what my mother and her stuck up friends think?" Carl was beginning to pant, his expression lost the slight, wry humor. It had turned very serious.

"Obviously not." Keith barely got the line out of his mouth. He was so hot he was about to come in his pants.

"Obviously not," Carl echoed softly. With slow deliberation, Carl drew Keith against him, wrapping one arm around Keith's waist, and another around his neck.

Grinding his hips against Carl's, feeling his enormous erection under his slacks, Keith levitated off the ground at the touch of their lips. Carl's tongue was fucking his mouth. Keith grabbed his face and sucked back, licking his lips and devouring him. "Oh, God..." Keith gasped as the fire consumed him.

"Troy! How could you!"

Hearing that dreaded line, Keith knew they were done kissing. This time he was determined not to screw up.

"I love this man! I don't give a shit who knows."

Betty pointed to Keith in horror. "You love him? What are you saying?"

Keith forced himself to stop swooning and pay attention.

"Yes! Okay?" Carl roared, "I'm gay! Now you know. So? Disown me? Beat me? What? I don't care. You won't separate us."

Betty let fly another smack at Carl's face.

Keith hated seeing him hit, even in an acting context. Straightening his back, Keith argued, "We're not gay. He's just my lawyer."

"Don't lie to me. I saw you kiss. What do you think I am, an idiot?"

Carl grabbed Betty's arm and led her off the patio. "You listen to me, Mother. You can't tell me what to do. I'm a grown man."

"Cut!"

"Excellent boys. Very nice, indeed!" Charlotte yelled with her eyes on the monitor.

Carl walked back over to Keith, swaggering proudly. "You were helpless in my arms."

"Was not." Keith sure as shit was.

"Oh? Didn't find your sticky fingers on my crotch this time."

"I decided not to."

"You were on another planet."

"You wish!" Keith wanted to hop on him and hump him.

"Okay. That one will do, boys. Nice job."

Carl grinned wickedly at him. "You better behave. I have another scene to do and I don't want you distracting me."

"What am I going to do? Flash my dick at you?"

"Don't you dare!" Carl wagged his finger at him.

Keith puffed up his chest and pressed against Carl's. "Who you ordering around? Hm? Big guy?"

When Carl grabbed Keith's jaw and kissed him, for real, Keith knew they were not alone. Far from it. Pushing back he choked, "What are you doing?"

The look of complete devastation on Carl's face cut through Keith like a knife. But Keith didn't want anyone thinking he really liked Carl. Not here. "I was just teasing, Carl. Can't you tell the difference?"

"Obviously not." He repeated the line from their script but it was tinged with spite.

When Carl stormed away, Keith felt sick. "Oh God." He didn't want to upset him. He needed him. For fuck's sake, he loved him.

101

Ken approached him to powder his shine. "You okay?"

"No. I fucked up." Keith bit his lip trying not to cry.

"Don't sweat it. The guy's nuts about you."

Keith stopped Ken and made him meet his eyes. "Did he tell you that?"

"He doesn't have to." Ken brushed Keith's hair.

As he was attended for his next scene, Keith watched Carl's performance. The man was so charismatic he upstaged everyone in the room. The anger Carl was evincing was like striking a match to dead wood. He was always on fire. Pausing to listen to his dialogue in complete awe, Keith wanted to own him, to possess him in ways he had never imagined wanting another person. "I'm insane."

Ken chuckled softly. "No. You're human."

Keith gave him a soft smile in reply.

When Carl had finished his scene and it was Keith's turn to act with another cast member, Keith waited as Carl attempted to storm past him. Grabbing Carl's arm, Keith stopped him. "I'm sorry."

"You have nothing to be sorry about."

"No. You're wrong." Keith swallowed the lump in his throat. "We have that sex scene coming up. I don't want you upset with me."

"I'm not. Don't be silly."

"You sure?"

"Yes. Go do your scene with Marty. Go on. Concentrate."

Checking Carl's eyes, making sure, Keith headed to the set to continue filming the episode.

Carl felt so guilty for putting Keith in that position he was furious with himself. What was he thinking? Kissing him like that in front of the cast and crew? He had no doubt the leak would ooze out into the tabloid press. How did you swear fifty people to silence with a piece of meat that juicy? He had basically just sealed their fates.

He hadn't meant to. They were flirting, teasing. It was just after they had caressed each other's crotch, kissed like they had never kissed another soul. The power of that contact, what it communicated to Carl was love, pure and simple. It made him ache.

Leaning against a wall, watching that blue-eyed, handsome blond show so much drama and passion as he performed, Carl was in awe of his talent. It was authentic. Obviously he had been well developed in the art of theater. His stage presence was huge, and his manner was natural charm.

"Oh, Christ." Carl brushed away a tear. "How can I fall for you? I'm such an idiot."

Keith finished his dialogue scene with Marty getting a renewed sense of nerves as he and Carl were going to be taking one another's clothing off for the next big love scene. Licking him. Keith was going to be licking Carl.

His skin broke out in chills.

They had a short break. Keith used the chance to slip to the men's room for a quick pee, and psych himself up while Carl was getting the shine powdered off his face.

Charlotte was waiting for them near the set of Carl's bedroom. Keith met her eyes for a moment and found her craning her finger at him. Feeling like a child about to get a scolding, he scuffed his leather soles to where she stood.

"Hey, babe," she whispered. "You doing okay?"

"Yes. Why?"

"I just don't want any tension showing between you two."

"No. There isn't. Don't worry." Keith figured she'd seen him push Carl away when he kissed him.

"It's been perfection up to now. We need to keep that edge."

"Yes. We will. Please stop worrying."

"Good. Go get into character."

Pivoting around, Keith found Carl already standing in his place waiting, watching him curiously.

"Get scoled?" Carl whispered.

"Yes. Never mind."

"Okay, you two love-birds," Charlotte shouted, "I'd love this in one take. I don't want any break in the action. But all I can ask is for you two to do your best. Will you do that?"

"Yes, Mother." Carl grinned sheepishly.

"More porn," Keith muttered out of the side of his mouth.

"Yup," Carl responded the same way.

"Right!" Charlotte backed up behind one of the cameras.

"Bedroom love scene. Take one. Action!"

Instantly Carl began shoving Keith's jacket off his arms. Battling with everything else on his mind, Keith made the transition from himself to Dennis Jason, and did it fast.

He wrapped around Carl's neck and kissed him, licking at Carl's tongue and closing his own eyes. Carl backed them up to the bed.

Keith's body was so keyed up, he knew they had lines as well and prayed they'd remember to say them.

"You gorgeous fucking creature," Carl hissed sensually. "I need you naked."

Keith's skin washed with chills. "I love you so much, Troy. Let's never let anyone tear us apart." Carl peeled Keith's shirt off, tossing it on the floor.

"No. Never." Carl pushed him back on the bed, tugging off Keith's shoes and socks quickly. Keith knew he had to start working on Carl's clothing as well, he just needed Carl to give him that chance.

When Keith was down to just his briefs, he grabbed Carl and dragged him down to the bed with him. Sitting up, Keith worked on Carl's shirt buttons with shaking fingers. Maybe Carl sensed his tension, Keith didn't know, but Carl began helping getting him undressed. Keith managed to get Carl's top half naked. Having to strip off his shoes, socks, and slacks, Carl stood off the bed. Keith had a momentary panic attack thinking Charlotte would shout out to cut the scene because Keith wasn't undressing Carl quickly enough. She didn't stop the action.

Jumping off the bed, Keith grabbed Carl's face and kissed him again as Carl stripped down to just his briefs. Once they were standing, facing each other, kissing, Keith felt more in control. Digging his hands through Carl's hair, sucking on his mouth, Keith felt Carl dig his hands into the back of his briefs, cupping his ass. It sent a charge of dynamite through him and he moaned and rubbed their dicks together through the cotton fabric.

Carl seemed to know they had to get going with more dialogue. Keith suddenly began to lose track of the time.

Gently Carl urged Keith to kneel on the bed. Once they were both on their knees, staring at each other, Carl said, "I want you to make love to me."

The intensity of Carl's stare made Keith's skin burn with fire. "I want that as well, Troy. With all my heart."

Leaning closer, Keith licked Carl's chest, running his tongue over his large pectoral muscle. A deep whimper vibrated under Carl's ribs. With Carl holding onto Keith's shoulders, Keith ran his tongue up his neck to his jaw and sideburn. Carl grabbed Keith on either side of his face and kissed him, dropping them down on the bed. He rolled over on top of Keith, still kissing him deeply and creating the most overwhelming sense of heat Keith had ever felt in his body.

As Carl pressed his hips into Keith's, connecting two very erect cocks, Carl leaned back on his arms to stare at him.

The gaze sent the tears rushing back to Keith's eyes instantly. It was so filled with adoration, it did indeed turn Keith to mush. "Oh God, I love you!" Keith gushed his last line before the end of the scene.

Carl fell back on top of him, kissing him, digging his hands into Keith's black briefs, dragging them down his hips as if he meant to tear them from his body.

"Cut!"

Carl parted from his mouth. They were both panting and sweating.

Before Carl climbed off him, Keith caught that look in his eye again. Not acting. No way.

Slowly Carl inched away from Keith to sit up on the bed with his back facing the camera to compose himself.

A woman with a sheet rushed in to give them privacy.

Clearing his throat, his hands covering his eyes, Carl shouted to Charlotte over the blind, "Any good?"

"Beautiful, boys. Very touching."

Keith watched as Carl exhaled a deep sigh in what could have been relief. Scooting off the bed, Keith picked up his slacks and stepped into them, fastening them as Carl did the same. The woman with the sheet lowered it and walked away.

"Well done. That's it for you two today. Great work, guys."

Keith followed Carl to the wardrobe area and they changed in silence.

Trying not to lose himself in the last scene, Carl dressed with his back facing Keith, his mind racing and blank at the same time. The amount he wanted those sex scenes to be real was gnawing at him.

Straightening out his expression, Carl noticed after they had finished changing that the next episode was being handed out. Hurrying to get his copy, he held it in his fingers and flipped the pages anxiously.

Keith leaned against his side. "More kisses?"

"I haven't found any yet." Carl wanted more. "Oh, thank fuck." He found a kissing scene. Tingles washed over his skin.

Keith looked at it from his side. "Is it a good one?"

Carl closed it quickly, like he'd been caught ogling a nude magazine. Keith laughed at him for his strange reaction and found his own copy. As they walked out of the studio to their cars, Keith stopped short.

Carl imagined he'd located the scene he was just reading. Opening the door for them to exit, he called out, "You coming?"

"It looks like she wants me to." Keith shook his head in disbelief. "I'm dressed, but we're kissing with your hands inside my jeans."

Smiling, Carl allowed him to pass first following him to his car. When they arrived at the Subaru, Keith leaned on the fender, reading.

Carl relaxed beside him.

"I can't believe they can get away with this on cable."

That made Carl smile again. "They can and they do."

"Wow."

Carl looked around the parking lot, watching people coming and going in the busy area.

Once Keith closed the script and tucked it under his arm, he faced Carl and whispered, "I'm sorry. I didn't mean to push you away like that earlier."

"You did the right thing. I was so fucking out of line."

"I just don't want anyone to know."

Carl focused on Keith's blue eyes. "Know what?"

"You know."

"No. Tell me. Know what?" Carl felt his heart pounding.

Keith scanned the area, replying shyly, "About us."

"Us? Is there an us?" Carl felt his body ignite, his cock go hard.

Those bashful light eyes had a hard time meeting his.

"Keith." Carl wanted to touch him. To cup his face and tilt it so Keith would look at him. "Please."

Keith tossed the script on the hood and hoisted himself up to sit on it. "I don't know."

Moving so he was leaning against Keith's knees, Carl urged, "I have to know."

Keith nudged Carl back so they weren't in contact, taking another paranoid look around.

"Sorry."

"It's okay." Keith rubbed his own legs with his palms nervously as if they were sweaty.

"I know you're afraid."

"Scared shitless," Keith muttered.

"You don't think I get that?"

"I thought it was bad enough I was pretending to be a gay guy on TV," Keith began. "If I see you as something other than a co-worker and a friend, then I am a gay guy. Not just an actor playing one."

"I know." Carl was dying. There was no winning this war.

"So, I can't see you as anything other than a friend and co-star."

"Fine." Carl twisted away to walk to his car. He figured that's what would happen. He shouldn't have had any expectations.

Watching Carl walk away was so hard, Keith felt that stupid lump form in his throat again. But someone had to be the smart one. How could they ruin two careers after one hit show? It wasn't sensible. Waiting until he could no longer see the taillights of the 'Vette, Keith slid off the hood and opened his car door. As he sat behind the driver's seat he punched the steering wheel in fury.

When he arrived home Keith tossed the script on the table with his keys and picked up the phone.

"Adam Lewis, can I help you?"

"Adam."

"Hello, Keith. I've been meaning to call you. I've got an offer for you to appear on Oprah."

"Oh. Cool."

"Is everything going all right? I'm excited about the new season. The premiere is coming up soon."

"Yes. It's actually going great. I'm loving the work and Charlotte is a kick in the ass."

"I've heard she's fantastic. I'm glad it's not a rumor."

"Speaking about rumors." Keith dropped down on the sofa.

"Oh? What about them?"

"Look, we've had this discussion before…"

"Keith, please stop worrying."

"No. This isn't the same question." Keith rubbed his face, running his fingers through his hair to his scalp.

"I'm listening."

Keith couldn't believe he was going to voice his concern to another soul, but Adam was gay, and his trusted agent. "If…if Carl and I—"

"Carl Bronson? Your co-star?"

"Yes. If Carl and I were to, you know, have sort of a relationship outside of work…"

"Relationship as in friendship, or as in lovers?"

Keith choked. He couldn't answer.

"Keith?"

He managed to croak out the word, "Lovers."

"I see…" Adam paused before he continued. "And? You want me to tell you if it'll be damaging?"

"Yes."

"Is it a fling? A one time thing? Or more?"

"It's not a fling. Actually, it's nothing yet."

"But if it was more?"

"Yes. If it was more."

Adam let go of a deep breath. "I wish I could say hurray, go for it."

"You can't?" Keith felt sick.

"Look, Keith, this is the strangest business on the planet. On one hand, it's liberal, open, accepting of alternate lifestyles, and to be honest, more men and women in this field are either gay or bi than anyone realizes. But…"

"Why is there always a but?"

"There are some men who have come out, who have claimed later that it has ruined their careers."

"That's exactly what I thought."

"I can't say for sure if you and Carl got involved that way, if the same thing would happen to you both. You're young, gorgeous, and have a whole career ahead of you. But saying that, if it does make a difference and the public rejects you, then your long careers will be a bit shorter."

"I'm so fucked." Keith held back a sob.

"Oh, baby. Do you love him?"

"Yes." Keith squeezed out before his throat closed.

"I'm so sorry, sweetie. I wish I could pump my fist in the air and say go for it. But if you do decide to have an affair, just be discreet. No one needs to know. It's not anyone else's business."

"Come on, Adam. Us just being a couple on the show kissing is enough to send the tabloids gossiping."

"I'm sorry, Keith. I think you have found the same dilemma that has cursed all same sex couples since the dawn of religion."

"You and Jack seem to be okay."

"Yes. We are. And friends of ours who work at an advertising firm are out as well. But none of us is in the public eye. We don't count on opinion polls for our paychecks."

"I know Charlotte is hoping we'll get together to boost ratings. So? How can that be bad?"

"It will. For her show. But when that show ends, or is cancelled and I try and find you new work, then what?"

"Come on, Adam. Are you telling me no one would hire me if I was an out gay man?" It was breaking Keith in half.

"No one outright states that fact, Keith. They just choose someone else who doesn't have a gay reputation in the tabloids."

"Augh!" Keith cried in agony.

"Just be discreet! Is it so difficult to see this man on level that's not public? No one knows who the hell you even are at the moment, and Carl is just starting to be recognized. Don't go public. Just meet in your own homes. That's not that difficult. Is it?"

"And deny it."

"Yes. Deny it like it's ludicrous. I'm telling you, you are not the first nor will you be the last, who has hid his true preference from the world. Look at Richard Chamberlain. He didn't come out until he was in his sixties."

"Richard Chamberlain is gay?"

Adam laughed, "What planet are you from?"

"Okay, Adam. I suppose I heard what I expected."

"I'm surprised you're asking me this for real. I never would have thought you could be gay."

Keith felt so embarrassed he was ashamed. "I didn't intend on it, Adam. Believe me."

"Do you guys do a lot of physical scenes? Love scenes?"

"God yes. Charlotte's got us all over each other."

"Carl is really hot. You'd have to be a robot not to want him."

"And he's so damn nice. Adam, I'd be lost without him. He's been my saving grace."

"That is wonderful to hear. Wait a minute. Don't you have a girlfriend?"

"Yes. That's another problem."

"Baby, life as a gay man is very complicated. Believe me."

"It seems silly. Why should it be complicated? We just love each other. What's the big deal?"

Adam laughed sadly. "I wish I knew the answer to that question. If you learn it, please pass it on to me."

"Thanks for listening, Adam."

"No problem. I'll email you the appointment time and place for your interview taping."

"Great. See ya." Keith hung up and deflated against the cushions. "I knew it."

Chapter Ten

The week had gone by quickly with rehearsals keeping him very busy. As Keith was going through his morning routine, the phone rang. Checking the time, knowing Patty was still sleeping, he grabbed it quickly. "Hello?"

"Hey. It's me."

Keith shivered at the deep tone of Carl's voice, but the quality sounded off. "You okay?"

"Yes. Look." Keith heard Carl take a deep draw of breath before he spoke. "Tonight the show premiers."

"I know." Keith walked away from the bedroom Patty was in so he wouldn't wake her.

"I was going to have a group of my friends over to watch it."

"Okay." Keith really thought Carl sounded strange.

"But I don't want a crowd tonight."

"So don't invite anyone over."

"I thought maybe you'd want to hang out with me. I'd like someone to come over and keep me company. I just don't feel like having to be the life of the party."

Upset with the sound of stress in Carl's voice, Keith agreed, "I'd be glad to hang out with you."

"I figured it'd be easier if you just followed me home in your car after today's rehearsals."

"That's fine." Keith checked his watch.

"Am I fucking up your own plans?"

"No. I don't have any. My parents wanted me to come over and watch it with them, but I said no. I didn't want to be in the same room with them when they figured it out."

"What about Patty?"

Keith looked back at the closed door. "I don't think she gives a shit. She never even commented about it."

"Fine. See ya at the studio."

"Okay. See ya." Keith hung up and looked at the phone for a moment. "What the hell is eating you, Carl?"

Carl finished getting ready, grabbing his car keys and wallet, stuffing them into the pockets of his black jeans. After Keith had pushed him away from their kiss and made it very clear he did not want the pretend relationship overlapping real life, Carl decided he was right. It was for the best. Carl didn't want a gay relationship anyway. It was too complicated. There were so many obstacles and traps about being a gay actor. It just wasn't worth it. This attraction to Keith was just some trick caused by the pretend one. Yes, it was nice to touch Keith, to kiss him, but Carl knew it was nice to touch a warm body, period. He'd been out of the dating game too long. By now he should have a woman living with him, be thinking about marriage and children. He was thirty, for crying out loud.

Closing the door to his condo, heading down to the garage, Carl elevated the garage door and sat in his car. They'd have dinner in, open a bottle of champagne to celebrate, watch the premiere, and that was it. Keith would leave.

Starting the car, knowing what the next episode entailed, Carl drove to the studio, trying to remember to keep his character, Troy Wright, separate from his real life.

Keith found a pad and wrote a note for Patty. I'll be watching the premiere with some of the cast. Be home late.

He set it by the coffee machine, knowing she'd find it there. Looking back at the empty living room, Keith left, a heaviness weighing him down inside.

After parking in the studio lot, Keith twirled his key ring around his finger absently, speaking the lines he had learned from the new script in his head as he approached the door.

Moving through the large building to the set, Keith located the group of cast and crew all chatting together and sipping coffee. Carl was seated out of the way, his script on his lap.

Keith imagined walking up behind him like he had done before, leaning his chin on his shoulder to snuggle. If he did it now, he'd be the worst hypocrite.

Instead, he stood over him, still spinning his key ring on his finger nervously. "Hey."

Without looking up, Carl replied in monotone, "Hey."

Keith knew he'd fucked with this man's head and he hated it. "Thanks for inviting me over tonight. I imagined watching it with Patty, or not watching it with her. She's irritated with me at the moment."

"Hm." Carl didn't look up. He kept reading the script on his lap.

"Carl?"

"Yes."

"Will you look at me?" Keith was ready to either slap him or cry.

With reluctance, Carl gradually raised his eyes from his script, to Keith's crotch, to his gaze.

"Please don't hate me."

"I don't hate you."

Keith's lip started to tremble and he felt like a moron instantly. "You mean a lot to me."

"You mean a lot to me too."

"I love this work. I don't want to be cut out of the script."

"What makes you think you'll be cut out?"

Glancing over his shoulder quickly at the rest of the crew, Keith turned back and replied, "If our chemistry dries up. If we don't light Charlotte's fuse…"

With a stern expression to his face, Carl asked in annoyance, "Why exactly would our 'chemistry dry up'?"

A sob about to burst from his throat, all Keith could say was, "Carl…"

"Okay people!" Charlotte clapped. "Speed read time!"

Keith backed up as Carl stood, brushing past him as he walked to the group.

Biting back his emotions, Keith swallowed hard and followed him.

They stood in a circle. Most of the cast had the scripts elevated in the air to read. Keith already had his memorized and suddenly felt as if he were rubbing everyone's noses in it.

Imagining them all growing to hate him, to plot behind his back to have him cut from the show, Keith battled with his paranoia to concentrate and speak his lines when appropriate. As Carl read, even the most sensuous and loving dialogue, he never met Keith's eyes, and just stared at the paperwork in his hand.

The next episode was mostly conversation and little else between them. Some kisses, no love scenes. They were setting up the pre-trial drama for the blackmailing, and Keith wanted them to get back to loving in Troy's big bed.

Carl was miserable. All he wanted to do was resume their fun flirting banter. But somehow he'd crossed a line and upset Keith. He couldn't bear to do it again. He loved Keith too much to make him uncomfortable, and would die if he lost him as a friend. Carl knew if he stared at Keith while he spoke his lines, he'd lose it. Cry like a baby and embarrass himself.

He just wanted to get through the day, go back to his place with Keith, and talk quietly about the premiere. They were friends. That's what friends did.

The time passed too slowly. Keith wanted to talk to Carl in private but Carl wasn't giving him the opportunity. Every time Keith made a move to whisper to him, Carl seemed to find someone to ask a question about the script, the blocking, the action, anything but let Keith say something in confidence. Keith couldn't wait until evening when he'd get his chance. This was making him very uncomfortable for so many reasons. The last thing he needed was for his career to be cut short before it began.

Finally they were released for the day. Keeping his eye on Carl as they left the building for the parking lot, Keith caught up to him and grabbed his elbow. Carl stopped short and looked down at their contact.

"You sure you want me to come over?"

"Not if you don't want to." Carl gently pulled back from Keith's grasp.

"I want to."

"Then follow me." Carl kept making for his car.

A cold pit developed in Keith's stomach again from the attitude. He preferred it when they acted like they liked each other. They were actors, couldn't they pretend they did?

Keith hugged the back of Carl's Corvette as if he were a horny dog sniffing his ass. They pulled into the parking lot of a tower condominium block. Keith parked in the guest area and walked down to the gated garage where Carl was waiting, keeping the metal grill from closing.

Keith wondered how lush the condo was. It certainly had to beat his crappy two-bedroom apartment.

In silence they ascended to Carl's floor in the elevator. Carl exited without a backwards glance and opened his door. Keith stepped inside and wasn't floored by the extravagance. It was a pleasant place but not a multimillion dollar penthouse. Out of a sense of duty he said, "Nice."

"Thanks." Carl tossed his keys aside and kicked off his shoes. "Hungry?"

"Yes. You?"

"A little."

"Carl, at least give me some damn eye contact when you talk to me. You've been avoiding looking at me all fucking day."

In reaction Carl slapped his palms on the counter of the island separating them and glared at him.

"Jesus!" Keith winced at the anger. "What the hell am I doing here, Carl?"

"I don't know. Why don't you fucking go home?" Carl opened the refrigerator and gazed in.

Biting his lip, not wanting to, Keith asked awkwardly, "Do you really want me to?"

"No." Carl took out a platter of cold shrimp and set it on the kitchen table.

"That looks like enough food for a group. I have a feeling I was a last minute decision." Seeing Carl's light colored carpet, Keith took off his shoes while he stared at the food.

"You were. I just decided I couldn't stand the idea of playing host. It's too draining." Carl pulled the plastic off the top of the tray. "Dig in."

Keith washed his hands at the sink and dried them, keeping his focus on Carl as he set out tall fluted glasses for champagne and more hors d'oeurvres. Sitting at the table, Keith dipped a large shrimp in cocktail sauce and bit it. "Mm. Fantastic."

"I'm glad."

"Here. Taste." Keith dipped one and stood, holding it in front of Carl's mouth.

He hesitated for a moment before allowing Keith to feed him. As he chewed he said, "That is good. Fresh."

A tingle passed over Keith's body. It felt a little more normal for a moment there. He reached for another shrimp as Carl set out plates and silverware. "Open." Keith dangled the crustacean in front of Carl.

"I can get my own. Sit down. Enjoy."

"Last one." Keith wanted to put it inside Carl's mouth.

Carl leaned closer, opening his lips.

It was so sensuous Keith almost combusted on the spot. Behaving himself and not jumping on him, Keith fed it to Carl.

"Thanks."

"My pleasure." Keith wiped his fingers on a napkin and finally sat down again, his cock rock hard in his jeans. "There's a lot of food here."

"I know. Whatever's left over I'll bring to work tomorrow."

"Good idea. Is everyone getting together?"

"I heard a few murmurs of gatherings. I didn't listen very closely. Can you imagine Betty and Marty at a party? Drunk off their asses?"

Keith laughed. "Uh, no way. I wouldn't want to see that."

"I have. It ain't a pretty sight." Carl held up the champagne. "Now? Or later?"

"Up to you."

"Now." Carl wrapped a towel around the stopper.

Watching Carl's biceps harden and swell as he forced the top off the bottle, Keith was so hot he wanted to attack him. It just seemed wrong somehow after the way he had pushed Carl off him. But here they could be discreet. Like Adam had said, if they just were private about it, why not play?

A loud pop sounded and Carl held the bottle over the sink as it gushed.

"Looks like it's coming," Keith chuckled.

Carl glanced over his shoulder at him. It was so sexy Keith knew he wanted him. Badly. "Perv," Carl teased.

Smiling, seeing a little spark of the old Carl there for a split second, Keith craved more. "Speaking about perving. What's with all the stupid dialogue lately?"

"The plot. Remember the plot?" Carl poured two tall glasses of champagne.

"Screw the plot. People aren't watching Forever Young for the plot."

"Oh?" Carl handed Keith a glass.

"No. They're watching it to see the sex scenes. You do realize Cheryl flashes her tits an awful lot when her and Omar are doing it."

"She loves it."

"Toast?" Keith held up his glass.

"To?" Carl waited.

"To us? To our debut of season two. Long may we run."

"To us." Carl tapped his glass and took a sip.

"Mm. Nice. You really know how to pick good food and booze. The last bottle of champagne I tasted was so nasty I couldn't drink it."

"Cheap champagne is unpalatable."

"I could never afford anything else."

"You get your first paycheck yet?"

"No."

"You will soon. Buy a nice bottle with it."

"I'll be paying bills with it."

Carl joined him at the table, eating more shrimp. "I remember those days. So, I should say, been there, done that."

Keith licked his lips as he watched Carl devouring the shrimp. "I know eventually I'll want to move out of that ratty apartment."

"I would think so. What about your girlfriend?"

Keith's smile vanished. "She's not my girlfriend."

"Oh?"

"Shut up. I told you about it. Don't act like you're an idiot."

"Am I doing that?" Carl licked his fingers and drank more champagne.

"Yes. I don't want to talk about Patty. Okay?"

"Okay."

"Feed me a shrimp."

"Why? Your hands broken?"

"I just want you to."

Slouching back in the chair, Carl tilted his head at Keith quizzically. "I don't know what you want. You confuse me."

"I want you to feed me a shrimp. Why is that confusing?"

Carl dipped one of the jumbo shrimp into the red sauce, and held it up. When Keith went to bite it, Carl drew it back mischievously. They played that game for a few minutes until Keith grabbed Carl's wrist and held it in place.

As he opened his mouth and pulled Carl's hand closer, Keith gazed at Carl's green eyes. Carl's concentration was on Keith's lips. Keith met Carl's fingers as he held the tail, and bit down, brushing his mouth over his sticky hand.

"You fucking cock tease," Carl's deep voice rumbled.

Keith smiled wickedly, chewing his food.

Taking his glass from the table, Carl reclined back on the chair, sipping it and staring at Keith as he did.

After consuming too much gourmet food and booze, they relocated to the living room to rehearse their lines. Carl was angry at himself because he still needed to use the script while Keith seemed to have it down pat.

"Wait…where was it again?" Carl searched the paperwork he was holding.

"You come in after I say, 'That woman set the whole thing up. She's notorious for blackmailing men, detective, and she can be trapped given the right opportunity'."

"Yes. I see it." Carl lowered the page and closed his eyes, fighting his urge to peek back at the lines.

"Let me wear a wire. Please. This never has to go to trial if I just have a chance to meet with her." Keith added, "The next line is Brian's. He says, 'It's not worth the risk'."

"Jesus! Did you memorize the whole thing?" Carl gaped at him as Keith sat on the couch while he paced nervously.

"No. Just my scenes."

"Right. My line is…" Carl searched the paperwork.

"I don't want to take a chance with my lover. That woman is insane."

Carl gave Keith a leering glance. "I can't believe you even learned my lines."

"They are my cue."

Carl hid the paper behind his back. "I don't want to take a chance with my lover. That woman is insane."

"Please. It's my only chance at clearing my name." Keith added, "Brian says, 'Is it so bad to be branded a homosexual?'."

Carl struggled to remember his next line. "I love him too much to put him through it, detective."

"Good!"

"Shut up," Carl chided. "You're distracting me."

"It's almost show time."

"Is it?" Carl asked in surprise checking the clock. "You're right." He dropped the script and found the remote control.

"Are you recording it?"

"Yes. I have the whole first series." Carl sat down next to Keith on the couch, pointing the remote at the television. "Want more champagne?"

"No. I'm already toast."

Carl glanced at him quickly, wondering why he couldn't tell he was tipsy. Muting the advertisements, Carl tucked one of his feet under himself and rested his arm on the back of the couch behind Keith.

"It's on."

Carl turned on the sound and hit record. The opening music began with the credits.

"There's my name!" Keith shouted, waving his arms in excitement.

Carl wanted to hug him he was so delighted.

Within the first few minutes of the show, their scene began. Carl heard his first lines of the new series with his handsome blond co-star.

"Dennis, Barry told me you're in trouble."

"I am. I'm sunk. My brother has been singing your praises. He said you're the best lawyer in the city."

"He's right."

"Can you help me?"

Carl felt his skin cover with goose bumps. Looking at the two of them together on the television, knowing how hot their love scenes got, Carl felt as if he were holding his breath.

"I think I can," Carl's character crooned.

"I'm serious, Troy. If you can't make this problem go away, I don't know what I will do."

"You just let me handle it. I owe it to Xavier to get you off the hook."

"Thanks, Troy. I mean that. I don't have too much money…"

"You don't worry about money, Dennis. We'll work something out."

As the scene broke and a commercial break intruded, Carl muted the sound and couldn't get over what they looked like together.

Peering over at Keith, staring at his profile while he sat still watching the dull advertisement, Carl had the urge to rest his hand on Keith's leg, but didn't.

Keith couldn't believe he was seeing himself on TV. It was as if it had to be someone else, and not him, saying those lines. It was absolutely the most mind-blowing experience he'd ever had. He, Keith O'Leary, was a star. A star on television! Wow.

"You okay?"

Beaming at Carl, Keith replied, "I'm more than okay. This is unbelievable."

"That's you, babe." Carl pointed to the television. "That's you on the TV being broadcast from coast to coast."

"I know! Shh. It's back on."

An hour later, Carl shut off the video recorder and sat back as scenes from next week played quickly. A tiny blip of them hugging and kissing was spliced into a montage of clips from the next episode.

Keith felt his heart racing at the excitement he felt. When Carl held out his hand to him, Keith took it.

"Well done. You were fantastic."

"Thanks, Carl. I owe it all to you. Honest. Without your support I'd have lost it."

Smiling warmly, Carl opened his arms.

Keith reached for that hug. Wrapping around him, inhaling him deeply into his lungs, Keith squeezed him tight. "Thank you."

"You are very welcome." Carl rubbed his back lightly, comforting.

Keith closed his eyes and pressed his chest against Carl's. The scent of Carl's aftershave and skin were intoxicating. Moving his hand to the nape of Carl's neck, Keith brushed his lips along the curve of Carl's rough jaw. Very slowly, Keith licked him.

He felt Carl tense up.

Keith had been imagining it all night, touching him, tasting him, but didn't find the courage. Watching them act together on the set, feeling Carl's arms around him, the champagne making him heady and light, Keith couldn't stop himself.

Running his tongue up Carl's throat to his ear, across his cheek, drawing a wet line to his lips, Keith connected to Carl's mouth finally. Thank fuck!

Carl responded, cupping the back of Keith's head, digging through his hair. As Carl slipped his tongue into Keith's mouth, the phone rang. Keith imagined it was Carl's friends calling about the show. Carl never made a move to answer it. What he did was push Keith back on the couch and press his hot, hard body against him.

Lying helpless under this fantastic man's weight, feeling Carl's stiff cock grinding on his, Keith wanted to weep he was so relieved. Lavishing in the dancing of their tongues, feeling so much love and respect for Carl, Keith whimpered in longing and knew he would never get enough of him.

Panting, Carl sat back to see Keith's face.

Keith touched Carl's skin with his index finger, tracing his features delicately, wanting him, needing him.

"Keith?" Carl swallowed audibly.

"Yes?" Keith answered in a dreamy lovesick way.

"What exactly does this mean?"

"It means I want you."

"Want me to do what?"

"Do what you want."

"To you?" Carl's voice sounded painful as he forced out words. "Do what I want?"

"Yes…" Keith pushed his hips up against Carl's.

"Please don't fuck with me, Keith, I can't take it."

Seeing the agony in Carl's sea green eyes, Keith cupped his jaw. "We need to be discreet. Only in private."

"Yes." Carl gulped the air as he struggled to control his breathing.

"No more kissing and playing in public or on the set."

"Yes. I know."

Keith spread his legs wider, smiling in invitation.

"Oh, Christ! I don't know where to start!" Carl choked with a sobbing laugh.

Keith began opening the buttons of Carl's shirt.

The moment Keith opened it, Carl shrugged it off. As Keith ran his palms up Carl's rippling muscles, Carl grabbed his right hand and kissed it, sucking each finger into his mouth to savor.

Feeling the velvety, wet heat of Carl's mouth giving each digit amazing head, Keith felt the swoon of pleasure washing over him in earnest. "Holy Christ, Carl…"

Carl focused on Keith's middle finger, sucking it deep into his mouth, running his tongue around it.

Keith was so hard he was in agony and needed to release his cock from the tight spot in his jeans.

Removing Keith's finger from his mouth, Carl dried it

tenderly in his hand and dropped back down to Keith's lips again.

While they kissed, Keith reached down Carl's tightly packed abdomen to the top of his jeans. Pushing the button through the hole, Keith parted the denim. Moving to the zipper, Keith dragged it down. Once he had Carl's jeans open, Keith slid his hand down his pelvis and into his briefs.

Carl let out a tantalizing moan of pleasure as Keith's hand came closer to his hardened cock.

Wanting to kiss but losing his breath from the excitement, Keith parted from Carl's lips and gasped for air. He hadn't touched Carl's cock yet, but just the feel of the hot, smooth skin of Carl's pelvis was driving him insane.

Carl pushed Keith's shirt up his torso, reaching under the material to cup Keith's chest, massaging his nipples.

A rush of lightning raced over Keith's body to his cock.

"Come to the bedroom." Carl slid off of Keith, reaching out his hand. The phone rang again. As Carl escorted Keith to the bedroom, he yanked the plug from the wall.

Standing in the dim, cool room, Keith couldn't stop panting. Carl, in only his open denim jeans, the hair on his lower abdomen dark and alluring, Keith felt his throat go dry at the attraction. It was so strong, Keith couldn't remember ever feeling this turned on before.

Meeting him in the middle of the room, Carl held the material of Keith's shirt and raised it up over his head. Keith's arms stretched to the ceiling and the shirt slipped off his body. Carl dropped it and went for Keith's zipper.

Staring down at his hands as he did, Keith was borderline hyperventilating again. No one was going to shout "cut" and end the scene. This was it.

Carl had to get him naked. He'd seen this man without clothing and knew how spectacular he was. Never expecting to be in his bedroom, undressing Keith O'Leary for real, Carl was high on the possibility of them actually having a relationship outside of work. He craved him, adored him, and was so sexually attracted to him it was making him lose sleep.

With his fingers in both Keith's briefs and jeans, Carl lowered Keith's clothing down his thighs. Instantly his engorged cock emerged and stood stiff and high.

"Oh, Keith..." Carl helped Keith step out of his clothes. Once Keith was completely naked, Carl sat back on his heels to take in the sight of him. "You are so fucking amazing."

"Carl..."

The cry was soft and nervous. Carl stood, wrapping around Keith to comfort him. Kissing his hair, he whispered, "We don't have to do anything you don't want to do."

"I know."

Carl cupped his face and kissed him again. As he did, he felt Keith's hands digging into his jeans, trying to lower them. Parting from his mouth, Carl took everything off his body and returned for more kisses.

Their naked lengths sealed together, swaying in a soft dance, Carl was in heaven. Gently, and with great care, they touched each other. Carl ran his hands down the silky skin of Keith's sides to his hips, as Keith cupped Carl's bottom pressing him from behind to connect their crotches.

After a long period of light, tickling caressing, Carl drew Keith to his bed. They lay side by side, continuing to touch, neither going towards the other's cock. Not yet.

Interspersed with their comforting stroking were kisses. Loving, soft, tingling kisses. Carl brushed Keith's hair back from his forehead, feeling his heat and dewy sweat. "Oh, babe. I'm in heaven."

"You feel really good, Carl." Keith smoothed his hand over Carl's chest.

"What do you want to do?" Carl whispered, kissing him after.

"Make love to you."

"Like in sex?"

"Not if you don't want me to."

"I want you to." Carl trapped Keith's jaw in his hands and kissed him again, slowly, making Keith moan in yearning.

"Do you have anything? You know. A rubber?" Keith asked sheepishly.

"I do." Carl wrapped around him again, rubbing his cock against Keith's leg.

"Or...do you want to do something else? Like ease into it?"

Carl parted from their embrace to see Keith's eyes. "Up to you."

Keith moved Carl back to look down at him.

As Carl held his breath, Keith finally made a move to touch

him where he wanted to be touched. While Keith appeared to be psyching himself up for the task, Carl pressed his hips forward into Keith's hand.

Keith couldn't believe he was touching Carl's dick. Watching Carl encourage him, pressing against his palm, Keith thought it felt very strange. It was as hard as his own, but seemed foreign, completely out of his comfort zone. He had to keep checking Carl's face, not only making sure Carl was okay with what they were doing, but to keep reminding himself that this was Carl. The man he was madly in love with. It was just so damn odd to touch a dick that wasn't his.

"That feels nice, Keith."

"Does it?"

"Yes."

Carl rested his head on his arm, lying on his side.

Growing slightly more confident, Keith wrapped his fingers around it. It throbbed in his hand. "You have a really big dick, Carl."

"Do I? I don't know what to compare it to."

"To me." Keith laughed.

"Bullshit."

"I can't believe I'm stroking another guy's dick."

"Do you hate it?"

"No. I don't hate it. I'm just not used to it."

"Can I touch yours?"

"Yes. I've been wondering why you haven't. I thought maybe the idea grossed you out."

"No. Not in the least. I just know neither of us has ever tried anything like this. I didn't want to overstep your limits."

"Maybe I was too bold to think I could just screw you." Keith watched as Carl's hand lowered to his cock. The minute it made contact he hissed with the shiver that raced up his spine. "Wow."

"It feels so nice." Carl explored Keith's dick slowly. "I get the oddest sensation that my touching your cock should make me come."

"I know. Like you can't feel your own fingers, and you're touching it anyway."

"Something like that."

"But it's not like that. You touching my dick feels so much

better than me jacking off. I'm fucking going nuts." Keith watched as a sticky drop dragged across Carl's knuckles.

"Do you like this?" Carl pressed his thumb into Keith's slit.

"Oh, Jesus. I know where to touch you and you know where to touch me." Keith did the move to Carl. A slippery drop oozed out under his thumb. He looked at Carl's face, his expression was pure passion.

Keith shimmied closer, keeping a tight grip on Carl's cock. "Let me fuck you. Please."

"I already said yes." Carl kissed him, using his tongue to trace across Keith's mouth.

"Get the rubber."

Carl pecked his lips and rolled off the bed. As he went, Keith pumped his own cock as he watched him walking around naked. If he kept it up, he'd come. He was ready to spurt from Carl's tender touch.

Carl returned with a rubber and a brand new tube of lubrication. After he rejoined Keith on the bed, Keith picked up the box. "You keep this handy around the house?"

"I bought it after we had our first love scene. So? You mad now?"

"No. Why should I be?" Keith urged Carl back on the bed and lay on top of him, pushing his knees to spread Carl's legs.

"Because I was hoping this would happen?" Carl caressed Keith's face.

"Then you are gay?"

"I suppose that's a moot point with a man shoving his dick against my back door." Carl laughed.

"You sure you're ready for this?"

"I'm sure. I've always heard if feels nice."

"Really? Up the ass?" Keith sat up and smoothed his hand over Carl's cock again.

"Yes. There's some pleasure center in there. I think it's the prostate."

"No kidding?" Keith opened one of the condoms with his teeth.

"I hope it's not a rumor." Carl took the cap off the gel and squeezed some out in his hand.

"I've never had a virgin." Keith grinned wickedly.

"Me neither. So wipe that smirk off your face before we switch places. Here." Carl held out the blob of gel. "Coat both you and me good, okay?"

"Of course." Keith picked up the goo in his fingers, rubbing it over the condom. "You want me to put some on your ass?"

"I can't exactly reach from here. Do you mind?"

"I suppose not since I'm going to be screwing it."

"Keith."

Keith paused, meeting Carl's eyes. Seeing Carl's furrowed brow, Keith answered his unspoken question. "Yes. I'm sure." Before he prepared Carl, Keith crawled over the bed to be face to face with him. "I'm absolutely mad about you, Carl. And the idea of us being one, me inside you, makes me so fucking hot I could come just thinking about it."

Carl cupped his face and kissed him. "I want you to. I feel the same way. I know it's insane, Keith." After he said that, he kissed Keith again. "And I want us to be united this way as well. I love the thought of your cock being inside me, believe me."

"Good. I can't wait. I can't imagine how it's going to feel."

Keith lowered back down Carl's body, sitting on his heels. Taking the tube of lube, Keith squeezed some on his fingers, and staring directly into Carl's eyes, he found his way between Carl's legs. With his fingertips on the rim of Carl's ass, Keith had to swallow for courage. It was just so damn alien for him. He'd only had sex with women. This was a trip to the moon and back.

Timidly, with his index finger, Keith smeared the slick gel around Carl's ring. Carl closed his eyes and his hips rose up in response. Keith couldn't believe his reaction. Biting his lip, Keith pushed the tip of his finger inside.

"Holy shit!" Carl choked in shock.

"Oh, no way. You have got to be kidding me."

"Push in!"

With more confidence, Keith pushed his one finger inside Carl.

"Aaahh!" Carl's cock bobbed and the veins showed in both his penis and his neck.

"Are you kidding me? It feels that good?" Keith thought he was acting.

"Put your fucking dick in me!"

"Holy fuck!" Keith felt the lust explode in his body at Carl's sudden desperation. Wanting him to be well oiled, Keith used more lube, rubbing it inside Carl's ass with more gusto.

"Auuugh!" Carl came, jerking his body and spraying cream

all over his chest.

Keith's jaw dropped to his chest. Kneeling up quickly, Keith put the head of his dick on target and stared in absolute wonder at the spattering of white puddles all over Carl's skin. Almost as if he couldn't restrain himself when offered a slick hole, Keith slowly moved his length inside Carl's body. The heat and tightness made his head spin. "Oh, Carl...oh, yes."

When Keith began pumping into him, deep and slow, Carl grabbed his own cock and jerked off like mad.

The sight made Keith explode with fire. "Again?"

Carl couldn't even answer. He arched his back and his hand became a blur.

Keith thrust into him harder, faster, watching Carl bring his body back up for the second orgasm.

Lavishing in the union, astonished by Carl's reactions to it, Keith came, pushing in to the hilt and hearing Carl's moaning grunts of pleasure as he climaxed once again.

Catching his breath, Keith was slightly shell-shocked, overwhelmed by intensity of the climax and the scent of male hormones rushing up his nose. Keith pulled out and gaped at Carl in astonishment.

Carl was floored. Rocking his hips side to side as the aftershocks ran over his body, he had never felt anything like that in his life. Exhausted, sated beyond his wildest dreams, Carl's chest was rising and falling rapidly and covered in his semen. "Keith...oh my God..."

Carl felt the bed shift and opened his eyes with effort. Keith was standing next to him, trying to pry the tight rubber off. "Still hard?"

"Yes. Jesus, Carl. Just watching you really blew my mind. Was it that good or were you exaggerating for my benefit?"

Carl started to laugh. "I'm not that good an actor!"

"I need to get this thing off."

Rolling off the bed, Carl followed Keith into the bathroom to wash up. Using a washcloth, Carl cleaned the come off his chest and the gel off his bottom. Keith managed to finally get the tight condom off. He tossed it out and took the washcloth Carl handed him. Once he was done, he met Carl's eyes.

Feeling so much love for this man, Carl wrapped around him.

"It was incredible, babe."

"Was it?"

"Oh, yes." Carl licked Keith's neck. "Was it nice for you?"

"It was. Carl, it was amazing."

Hugging him close, Carl caught Keith staring at their reflection in the mirror. "We look good together."

"We do." Keith pressed his cheek into Carl's shoulder.

Nestling into his hair, Carl asked, "Can you stay over? I bet it's nearing one."

"I suppose so. I don't think Patty will care."

"Do you want to call her?" Carl stood back to check on Keith's expression.

"No. She's definitely asleep by now."

"Come." Carl held his hand, shutting off the bathroom light.

Switching off lights as they went, Carl turned down the bed, setting the rubbers and lube on the nightstand. They cuddled under the covers, interweaving their legs and arms.

Keith rested his head on Carl's chest. "Did it really feel that good when I penetrated your ass?"

Carl laughed softly. "Keith, I never would have believed it."

"Huh."

Hugging him tighter, Carl kissed Keith's hair. "It makes me feel so close to you. Sharing that."

"Yes. It does. I always thought sex was supposed to do that."

"It doesn't always." Carl used his fingertips to run over Keith's back gently.

"No. That's the pity of most relationships. And it shouldn't be that way."

"Are you what you consider a traditional kind of man when it comes to that, Keith?"

"Yes, in some ways. I think sex is for people who love each other. And it was a mistake with Patty because we didn't."

Carl thought that sentence through. "You love me?" Waiting for Keith to answer, Carl felt him nestle closer. Keith's hand lowered to Carl's pubic hair. Feeling Keith cup his soft genitals affectionately, Carl felt his answer in the touch. "It's strange, Keith. There we are on a set telling one another we love each other, touching, kissing, and it seems so right. I don't feel as if I'm acting or lying. I honestly believe I am telling a person I am in love with, the truth."

Keith leaned on his elbows and stared down at him. Even in

the dimness Carl could see the glimmer in Keith's light eyes.

"Me too. But please. Let's just keep it quiet."

"I know, babe. You don't have to tell me." Carl brushed his knuckles over Keith's cheek.

Keith kissed him. "I hope I can sleep. I'm very excited by everything we've done tonight."

"Excited? Or nervous?"

"All of the above. It was all so new to me. And to you."

"But it was a nice newness. It felt refreshing to touch and be touched by someone you are so turned on by, so in love with." Carl smiled impishly, "Even if it was a man."

"Jesus. We screwed, Carl. Two men."

"I know. Wild, huh?"

"I'm lying here in your arms and I still can't believe I— we did that together."

"And it felt so good!" Carl wriggled against him, feeling his cock respond.

"Jesus!" Keith laughed. "Another hard-on?"

"Keith, you have no idea what that felt like. My God. It was ten times more intense with you inside me, than when I just orgasm on my own."

"I'm intrigued."

"Are you?" Carl drew him closer to his lips.

"Yes," Keith replied shyly.

Unable to resist, thrilled they had crossed over from a game of teasing to reality, Carl kissed him with all the love he could muster, wanting to show Keith how much he cared.

That kiss! Oh, Jesus, that kiss!

Keith knew they couldn't sleep. How on earth could they shut their eyes knowing the kind of pleasure they could give to each other?

Maneuvering back on top of Carl, this time, spreading his legs wide over Carl's hips, Keith replayed Carl's face in orgasm over and over in his mind, from the first one where Keith was just touching his ass, to the second one, when he was deep inside him. "I love you," Keith breathed between kisses, stoking both their passions.

Carl wrapped around him and rolled them over, so he was on top. Parting from Keith's mouth, Carl sucked at Keith's neck, licking his jaw and running his teeth over Keith's taut skin.

Shivering at the touch, Keith groaned and closed his eyes. The more they did, the more familiar and normal it felt. What had started out as churning fear and the sensation of unfamiliar sights and scents, had become a natural craving.

Carl began grinding his hips against Keith's, rubbing their cocks together as they stood stiff from their bodies.

"My God! You make me insatiable!" Keith gasped as another wave of chills coursed over him.

"Oh, babe…I know. I can't believe I feel this way about you. About a fucking man!" Carl laughed but it soon faded to a moan of passion.

"You? You can't believe it? I'm in shock."

"Does this shock you?" Carl stroked Keith's cock.

"God…" Keith's body spun from the intensity. "It should. I know it should."

"How about this?" Carl cupped Keith's balls.

Unable to fight the attraction to Carl, Keith grabbed his rough jaw and devoured him once again. As Carl's hands explored more boldly this time than earlier, Keith writhed in ecstasy against his hard body.

"We'll never get any sleep."

"I don't care," Keith whimpered, thrusting his hips into Carl's palm.

Carl parted from Keith's mouth, reaching for the nightstand.

Thinking he was going to get a rubber, Keith froze, his heart pounding wildly. *Can I do this? Take a man's cock up my ass?*

"Carl?"

"Don't worry, babe."

"But…" Keith held his breath.

"Hang on. Calm down." Carl sat between Keith's straddled legs with the tube of lube.

"Oh." Keith knew what he was going to do now. "Okay."

Carl leaned over to kiss him. "You need to trust me."

"I do. Honest."

"I'm not rushing you to do anything. You just have got to feel this."

"Yes. I want to. I saw what it did to you." Keith kicked the rest of the covers back, panting in anticipation.

"Oh, lover, you are going to die." Carl touched his fingertips to Keith's ass.

Keith tensed up and almost stopped Carl out of fear. As one finger slipped in smoothly, Keith's eyes opened wide in disbelief.

He heard Carl's soft laugh. "Wait. It gets better."

Clenching his fists from the nervous anxiety, Keith felt that finger stroking him inside.

"Agh!"

"Good or bad?" Carl stopped.

"Good!" Keith choked as he said it. "Holy fucking shit!"

"Hold onto your hat...or your cock, whichever."

Keith grasped his dick with both hands. He was in shock. "Deeper! Oh, Carl! Deeper!" I cannot believe I am telling a guy to push deeper into my ass! I have lost my mind!

Carl used two fingers, finding the magic spot. They both knew he had hit it, because Keith's hips elevated instantly and his hands jerked him off in a rush of movement.

Keith felt it begin deep in his balls and the rushing of the come to his cock was so intense he almost passed out. "Holy mother fucker!" he shouted, the come spurting out and hitting him in the jaw. Keith kept bucking like a bronco as Carl's fingers prolonged it to impossible lengths.

Gasping for air in astonishment, Keith blinked and found Carl jerking off again, intending on sending his own come onto the pile of creamy spatter.

Milking his cock as he watched, Keith couldn't believe how beautiful Carl looked during orgasm. "Oh my God..." he crooned while Carl's come pelted his skin.

Dropping back to his heels, Carl moaned, "God! I am so spent."

"We have got to get some sleep, Carl. We have to be at the studio tomorrow."

Groaning as he unfurled his legs stiffly, Carl climbed off the bed, stumbling to the bathroom.

As they went through the clean up routine again, Keith felt drained, yet sated.

Once they collapsed into bed, Keith wrapped around Carl and they instantly fell under the spell of sleep.

Chapter Eleven

The alarm buzzer woke Keith. Blinking, looking around the strange room, he felt the bed shift and found Carl slapping the snooze button on the clock radio. As Carl nestled back into the pillows for that precious five minutes, Keith stared at the ceiling light fixture and tried to think.

I screwed Carl Bronson last night.

That reality scared the living shit out of him. "What the hell am I doing?"

A cold chill passed over his skin with the worst morning after regrets he had ever imagined. The magnitude of that decision, the threat to his career, his family ties, his life, made Keith panic. This can never happen again. This has to be just some one-time thing.

The alarm buzzed again.

Carl leaned up and shut it off. Moving over to face Keith, Carl whispered, "Good morning."

"Uh, hi." Keith didn't look at him. He was mortified at what they had done. How could they have been so stupid?

Carl's hand smoothed over Keith's stomach. It made Keith flinch and cover with chills.

"Did you sleep okay?"

"Hm? Yes, fine."

Shifting his position, Carl leaned up higher to see Keith's face. "What's wrong?"

"Nothing."

"Keith," Carl admonished. "Are you freaking out about what we did last night?"

"Yes."

"Because?"

"Because we're so screwed if anyone finds out."

"Okay. But what about what it meant to us."

As Carl's hand caressed him lightly, moving up his chest, Keith shivered at his touch. Us? What it meant to us? Are we a couple? A fricken gay couple? Oh God.

"Keith." Carl shook him. "You have to tell me what's going on in your head."

Finally finding the courage to meet his gaze, Keith pressed his cheek against the pillows. It was a mistake to look at him. Carl was too gorgeous. His long, brown hair tussled from the night's rest, his green eyes illuminated by the sunlight pouring in from the window, his beard growth dark and masculine, Keith felt his body burn. "Oh shit."

"Oh shit, what? Keith, please. I'm dying here."

Keith leapt on top of him and pinned him underneath him. Brushing his lips over Carl's coarse sandpaper jaw, Keith closed his eyes and felt his morning hard-on throb against Carl's under him.

Carl wrapped his arms around Keith and hugged him. "I understand. This is freaking me out a little too. It's just so strange to feel these things for another man. It's giving me uncomfortable rushes of fear."

"Yes." Keith rubbed his face into Carl's hair, suppressing a shiver of terror.

"I suppose it's just because we're on day one. I assume with time it becomes easier."

Keith leaned up on his elbows to see Carl's eyes. "I feel like I might have a panic-attack about it later when I really think about what we're doing."

"I know," Carl chuckled softly.

"It's just that everything is happening to me at once."

"Yes. It must feel overwhelming." Carl pushed Keith's hair back from his forehead, but it fell back down to cover his eyebrows.

"What if someone figures it out? Carl, can we afford to take that chance?"

After a deep sigh, Carl replied, "I suppose we'll have to make a choice. Is what we have, our relationship, worth the risk? I mean, ultimately, that's the question. Could we, or should we, pretend we don't want to be together? Avoid each other?"

Keith didn't like that idea one bit.

"Is that what you want?" Carl asked.

"No." Keith breathed tiredly. "I don't want us to avoid each other. I know myself. I'd obsess over it."

"Would you?" Carl appeared amused, combing his fingers through Keith's hair lovingly.

"Yes." Keith connected to those green eyes, the gold ring around them glittering like a jewel.

"Then I don't know any other option, babe." Carl pecked his lips. "We hide our love. Simple as that."

"Simple?" Keith choked sarcastically.

"It could be. You and I are actors in the same show. We need to see each other, to rehearse, to learn our lines...so? We won't hold hands in public, won't kiss where a photographer could shoot it, and we try to continue pretending to be only just good friends. What's so hard about that? Aren't we trained pretenders?"

That made Keith laugh. "The great pretenders."

"Yes. Keith, we are not the first, nor will we be the last male actors to do this. We shouldn't be behaving as if we're writing the book or setting some precedent."

"I know. You're right." Keith fears slowly subsided.

"Let's just play the stupid game, Keith. Deny, deny, deny..."

"You sound like Adam Lewis."

"Oh? Did you have a discussion with him about us?"

Seeing Carl's impish grin, Keith felt his cheeks blush. "None of your business."

Carl peeked at the clock. "We have to get going, babe. Shower, and a quick cup of coffee. Do you have to stop home?"

"I should. I don't have a change of clothing."

"Want to borrow mine?"

"Gee, that won't look obvious." Keith rolled his eyes.

"Who the hell knows what shirts I own? Give me a break."

"You're bigger than I am!"

Carl pecked his lips. "Shower. Come on."

Keith reluctantly separated from Carl's body. Following him to the bathroom, he waited his turn as Carl relieved himself in the toilet. As Keith urinated, trying not to care that Carl was in the room, Keith peeked into the mirror to see him busy starting the water in the shower.

"I have a new toothbrush." Carl opened a drawer and removed one still in its package. "Help yourself."

"Thanks." Keith gave his dick a shake and found Carl had watched that action. Trying not to blush, knowing he was slightly shy about certain things, even with women, Keith leaned over the sink to wash his hands and brush his teeth. While he did, Carl climbed into the shower.

His mouth rinsed, Keith leaned back on the sink to wait. After a minute Carl shouted, "Aren't you coming in?"

"With you?"

"Yes! Get in here!"

Keith pushed back the door. Seeing Carl's crotch soapy and his dick standing straight up, Keith hurried in excitedly. "I thought we didn't have time."

"Save time. Shower with a friend."

"You sound like a bumper sticker." Keith stood under the crashing water. When Carl's hands began washing his genitals, Keith choked in surprise. "Jesus, Carl! That's not helping our close time frame very much."

"But it feels so nice." Carl slithered his fingers all over Keith's growing anatomy.

A swoon washed over Keith suddenly. He reached out to the wall and door and braced himself. Looking down, seeing Carl's hands massaging him with so much confidence and care, Keith's teeth ground in longing.

When one finger pushed its soapy way up his ass, Keith's breath caught in his throat and he jerked his hips forward in reflex. Clenching his jaw, his eyes sealed tight, Keith couldn't believe the pleasure rushing to his groin. "Oh, Christ, Carl..."

"Come for me, handsome."

Losing the feeling in his legs, with the water pelting his back, Keith gripped the handle on the shower door and almost passed out from the power of the orgasm. His deep, grunting whimper echoing off the wet tiles, Keith shot his load and struggled to open his eyes and function after.

"Do me. Come on. Quickly."

Shaking his head, trying to clear his foggy brain, Keith gazed down and found Carl stroking his own soapy, hard cock. Pushing his frightening doubts and trepidation to the back of his mind, he reached for Carl's dick as Carl released it and held onto the door and wall.

Sliding that length through his fingers and palm, Keith was still trying to get used to touching someone else's penis. How long would it feel odd? Would he eventually find this natural?

"Faster, come on," Carl urged.

Snapping out of his thoughts, Keith fisted Carl more

aggressively. As Carl's posture reacted and he thrust his hips out and tensed his muscles, Keith traced his gaze from Carl's face, erupting in pleasure, to his wet chest, hard nipples, soapy pubic hair and large engorged cock.

A choking grunt squeezed out of Carl's throat. His come spattered Keith's body, surprising him, because he didn't expect to get hit.

"Oh, babe...that was fantastic."

Rinsing off, finishing up quickly, Keith was hard again and wondered why, if this was so strange, did it turned him on so much?

After a quick sip of coffee Keith was racing over the roads to his apartment. Knowing the time was running short, he took the stairs two by two and opened his door quickly. Dashing to his room for clothing, he slowed down when he found Patty asleep in their bed. Tiptoeing, he removed clean underwear and a shirt from the drawer, left the room and changed in the living room. After tossing his dirty clothing into the hamper, he grabbed the script and his keys and was about to head out when he heard his name.

"Keith."

He spun around to see Patty's drowsy gaze.

"I'm incredibly late."

"Where did you sleep?"

"At Carl's. He had a big get together and I was too drunk to drive home." Why was the lying coming so easily?

"Your mom and dad called."

"Oh?"

"They wanted to congratulate you."

"Did they say anything...about..."

"No."

"I'll talk to you later. I really have to go."

"Okay."

He waved, racing out the door and back to his car. As he went he turned on his mobile phone and stuck it to his ear. His parents had left a message on it as well. It was light and sweet. No bad tone about the fact he was playing a gay man.

Keith shut it off, hurrying to get to the studio.

Carl checked his watch as the crew set up for the next episode's scenes. Sitting comfortably, Carl had the script on his lap but was staring through it, not reading it. Replaying the night over in his head, he was feeling a mixture of anxiety and fear. What would it be like now to have kissing and love scenes with Keith? Easier or harder now that they'd had intercourse?

Well, if Charlotte wants passion she'll certainly get it.

How would it appear to the rest of the cast and crew? Would they see the difference? Or had Keith and he already acted like they were attracted and it would appear the same? Carl didn't know what would be given away. How did you stop the loving glances? The adoring smiles? Those things were automatic when you're crazy about a person. And Charlotte was so damn smart, so perceptive...

Carl tapped his finger to his lips unconsciously as his thoughts grew deeper and his memories of Keith's body on his made his skin cover with chills.

"Carl?"

Jerking his head up to Charlotte as if she had been reading his mind and he was already guilty as charged, Carl replied, "Yes?"

"You have any idea what's keeping Keith?"

"I'm sure he'll be here at any moment. He's very conscientious."

"Did you guys watch the premiere together?"

There it was. Instantly Carl had to analyze what the answer would mean to Charlotte. He and Keith were co-stars and friends. It would seem perfectly natural for them to have been together last night. Why on earth was he reluctant to tell her they were?

"Hello?" She laughed, waving her hand in front of his face as his stare became lost.

"Sorry I'm late!" Keith rushed over, huffing from his run.

"Late night?" Charlotte asked with a wry smile on her lips.

Keith met Carl's eyes, as if checking to see what he should say.

Rubbing his jaw in anxiety, Carl had a bad feeling that this charade would crumble very quickly.

"Uh. No. Just overslept." Keith ran his hand through his hair nervously.

"Let's get moving," Charlotte ordered, pointing to the wardrobe area. "Change. Get ready."

Carl stood, touching Keith lightly on his shoulder to prod him in the right direction. Once they were walking, Carl looked back to see Charlotte staring after them for a minute before she got busy.

"Everything all right?" Carl asked quietly as he began changing clothing.

"Yes. My parents called last night. Patty said they didn't mention anything in particular about my role to her."

Nodding, Carl didn't want to continue the conversation with Melvin listening.

Dressed in their characters' clothing, they returned to the set and found two of their co-stars finishing up their scene. Carl stood back, watching them. Cheryl and Omar were sucking face, pawing at each other while Charlotte chewed on the end of a pen and scrutinized their every action.

Feeling Keith lean against him, Carl peered over at him. Keith was smiling affectionately at him. Carl couldn't prevent smiling back.

"You smell good," Keith whispered.

Knowing they were filming, Carl bit his lip on his chuckle.

"Cut!"

Carl exhaled a deep breath. The heavy petting on the set was very arousing. Charlotte certainly knew how to tantalize her audience.

"Are they a couple outside work?" Keith asked, still whispering softly.

"No. She's got a boyfriend from a daytime soap and Omar's single."

"When is he making that movie he's been cast in?"

"I think this summer, when we break for the season."

"He's so lucky."

Carl faced Keith who was staring at Omar as he listened to Charlotte's instruction. "You'll get there. Stop worrying."

"I hope so."

Carl had an overwhelming urge to kiss his cheek. It was murder not doing it.

"Where are my boys?" Charlotte roared.

"That's us." Keith hurried to meet her.

"Okay, my darlings…you ready for your scene?"

Carl noticed Brian getting his face powdered quickly.

"Yes, ma'am," Keith replied enthusiastically.

"This one's just a quickie. A few lines to set up the next

scene." Charlotte looked back at Brian. "You ready?"

He rushed over. "Yes."

Giving him a quick once over, Carl thought Brian was very handsome, perfectly cast as the police detective for the scene. When he broke his gaze he found Keith eying him suspiciously. "What?" Carl asked him.

Both Charlotte and Brian looked at Keith.

"I didn't say anything!" Keith threw up his hands, shooting Carl an annoyed glare.

"Okay. Go to your places." Charlotte backed out of the scene.

Buttoning the jacket of his suit, Carl tried to get in character and not let everything that was on his mind distract him, which proved harder than he thought.

After a silent moment to allow them to concentrate, someone shouted, "Detective scene. Take one. Action!"

Keith began, "That woman set the whole thing up. She's notorious for blackmailing men, detective. And she can be trapped given the right opportunity. Let me wear a wire. Please. This never has to go to trial if I just have a chance to meet with her."

"It's not worth the risk," Brian said.

Wrapping his arm around Keith, Carl replied, "I don't want to take a chance with my lover. That woman is insane."

"Please. It's my only chance at clearing my name." Keith ran his hand through his hair anxiously.

Brian paused, backing up as if looking at them as a pair. "Is it that bad to be branded a homosexual?"

"I love him too much to put him through it, detective." Carl met Keith's eyes and tried not to smile at his innocent expression.

"Let me get her to confess, please," Keith urged.

"All right. Let me talk to my superiors about it first. I'll get back to you."

"Thank you, detective." Keith shook Brian's hand and both he and Carl waited as he walked off the set.

After he had, Carl turned Keith to face him. "You are not to be placed in harm's way. I refuse to let you meet with that woman."

Keith's lips curled into a passionate smile. "I do love you for that."

Carl cupped his face and felt his eyes watering from the passion he really felt for Keith. He had to fight back the desire to gush out his lines like a moron in love. "If anything happens to you, I'll be devastated."

"It won't. Don't worry."

Carl wrapped around him and drew Keith's body to press against his. Opening his lips, Carl connected with Keith's mouth, and the kiss consumed him it communicated so much emotion.

Keith let out a lovely little whimper of yearning that sent Carl's cock upward.

"Cut!"

Gently parting from Keith's lips, Carl gave him his warmest glance. He forced himself to shake off the sensation of holding his true lover and get back to pretending he was acting.

"Nicely done, boys. Okay, next... Where's Betty?"

Carl walked off the set and tried to compose himself. Would each scene with Keith now set him off on an emotional tailspin?

Keith was still smiling. During their kiss he felt Carl's cock go rigid. How cool was that?

Pouring himself a glass of juice from the refreshment table, Keith sipped it, staring at him contentedly. When Carl caught his gaze, Keith smiled in excitement.

As if he were suddenly bashful, Carl lowered his lashes and walked over. "Hey."

"Hey," Keith crooned.

"That was so nice."

"Oh, yes. I hate it when she yells cut."

"Uh, what was with the dirty look earlier?"

"Dirty look?" Keith narrowed his eyes.

"Yes."

"Oh. I just thought the way you stared at Brian was a little strong. Are you attracted to him?"

"Jealous already?" Carl teased.

That surprised Keith. "No. Should I be?"

"You really are confusing me." Carl looked back at the scene being played out a few yards from where they stood.

"I don't mean to. I'm just so new at all this. I mean, are gay couples exclusive?"

Carl took a quick look around before he answered. "I suppose they are if they want to be."

"But two guys? How could two guys be loyal?"

"I don't get you? What do you mean how could two guys be

141

loyal?"

"Carl! Men cheat."

"Not all men cheat!" Carl appeared insulted.

"You know how many actors have relationships that last? Come on. Add to that, gay actors?"

"Can we discuss this later?"

"Yes, sorry. I just wondered about it since you gave Brian a good once over."

"I did not!"

"Did too!"

"Shh!" Someone hissed as their voices grew louder.

When Keith met Carl's eyes again, he found his smile. Keith laughed at their silliness and couldn't wait to get his hands on him again.

The shooting finished, the next episode in his hand, Carl stopped short and flipped the pages like a fan to see what was coming next. That lovely, familiar heat pressed against his side.

"Anything good?"

"Let me see…" Carl read a few lines. "I think we're going to get lucky again. I'm getting tired of too much dialogue and not enough sex."

Keith chuckled softly.

Closing the script, Carl met Keith's shining blue eyes. "Are you coming over?"

"I should stop home. I need to end this thing with Patty properly."

"You haven't done that yet?" Carl asked, gesturing for them to leave the building.

"Not formally."

Keith opened the door for them and they walked out into the sunshine.

"Do you want to come by after?" Carl needed him. Craved him.

"Can I let you know?"

"Of course." A little let down, Carl smiled warmly, trying to be supportive.

"We could always have phone sex." Keith's seductive leer lit Carl on fire.

"You did jerk off that time we were going over the script,

didn't you?"

The blush came quickly to Keith's cheeks.

"Naughty boy." Carl's cock was so hard he wanted to grab Keith and dry hump him.

"How embarrassing." Keith glanced around the parking lot as they stood near his car.

"Don't be embarrassed. It's making me hard as a rock."

Keith's eyes darted to Carl's black jeans.

"So, uh," Carl tried to get under control, "call me later."

"I will. Believe me, if I can come by, I will."

"Bring a change of clothing." Carl stuffed his hand into his front pocket so he could discreetly shift his dick and get comfortable. Keith appeared captivated by the act.

"I will."

"See ya later?"

"Hopefully."

Carl smiled and walked off, the friction of his tight denims rubbing his cock, arousing him as he did.

Keith tore his eyes away from Carl's ass and the memory of being inside it. Sitting down behind the wheel of his car, he set the script on the passenger seat and started the car. Before he drove off, he reached into his pants and did the same thing, moving his cock upright where it could lie flat against his pelvis. *You gorgeous son of a bitch. I have got to see you tonight.*

Less than an hour later Keith parked and headed inside his apartment building. Coming through his door, he tossed his keys and the script down and noticed the message machine light blinking. Hitting the play button he heard his mother's voice.

"Shit." He picked up the phone and dialed their number.

"Hello?"

"Hi, Mom."

"Keith! You were wonderful in the show. I am so proud of you."

Keith waited for the inevitable. "What did Dad think?"

"He thought you were great."

"You sure?"

"You mean because you play a gay man?"

"Yes." Keith swallowed his anxiety.

"Why would that matter to your father, Keith? It's acting. It's a role. He liked Will and Grace."

Rubbing his forehead, Keith asked, "Oh?"

"Yes. He thought that show was very amusing. Keith, don't worry. No one will think you're a gay man simply because you play one on the television."

"No. Of course not." Keith felt sick to his stomach.

"The important thing is that you are working and you have been cast in a fantastic show. I bet this year it gets nominated for an Emmy."

"I hope so. That would be great."

"Did you ask Patty when would be a good time to come out for a meal with us?"

"Look, Mom, Patty and I are kind of in the process of splitting up."

"Oh, that's too bad, honey. I thought Patty was a very sweet girl."

"She is. I suppose we just don't love each other." Keith stared at the cover of the new script as he spoke. "I just don't know what to do about the living situation."

"That is awkward. Do you want to come back and live at home for a while?"

"Not really." Keith laughed to soften the blow. "But I appreciate the offer."

"What will you do?"

"I don't know. I wish I could find her a new roommate. She's struggling financially and that's not helping me make a decision at the moment."

"Yes. I can understand."

"Anyway..." Keith stood. "Let me go. I have to get busy learning the new episode."

"Okay, Keith."

"Tell Dad I said hi."

"I will. And once again, congratulations, honey. We're very proud of you."

"Thanks." Keith hung up and muttered, "You wouldn't be proud of me if you knew I was screwing your newest heartthrob."

Picking up the script, Keith began reading it, sitting down on the sofa. Finding another hot love scene between him and Carl, he read the notes eagerly and felt his body respond. Pausing, Keith lowered the pages and imagined it in his head. Carl's hands all over his body, Carl's mouth on his, the scent of his cologne and skin, the heat of his cock pushing against his own.

Closing his eyes, Keith tried to calm down. Slapping the script on the cushion next to him, he picked the phone back up and dialed.

"Hello?" a rushed Patty answered.

"Can you talk?"

"For one second. It's busy here."

"I…I was going to spend the night at a friend's place."

"Here we go."

"Patty, we know this isn't going anywhere."

"Can't this wait 'til I'm home?"

"Well, not really. I'll be gone by the time you get home."

"Keith…" she moaned.

"Listen to me." He knew he didn't have much time. "I won't move out until we get another roommate for you. I promise. But I can't keep pretending we have some kind of committed relationship when we don't."

"Fine. I'm really busy."

"I'm sorry, Patty. You know how much this hurts me?"

"Not bad enough if you already have a new girlfriend. Who is it? Your co-star? Cheryl Jones?"

Stifling a choking denial, Keith replied, "I'm sorry it didn't work out between us, Patty. Honest I am."

"Whatever. I have to go." She hung up.

He looked at the phone and disconnected the call. Composing himself after the guilt consumed him, Keith dialed Carl's number.

"Hello?"

"It's me."

"Hiya, babe."

"Can I come over?"

"Do you have to ask?"

"Be there in a half hour."

"Can't wait."

Keith rose off the couch, hung up the phone, and headed to his bedroom to pack a small bag of things he needed. He couldn't help it if things didn't work out between him and Patty. Relationships ended all the time. She didn't love him. Patty didn't show him the kind of passion Carl did, or look at him with her eyes filled with excitement the moment he stepped into a room. Her touch didn't cause him to get so hard he was ready to combust. No. He and Patty did not have what he and Carl had.

But he wasn't to blame. These things just happened.

Carl jumped to his feet after he hung up the phone. "Yes!" he cheered, setting the script down on the kitchen table and straightening up the condo quickly. When the phone rang again he hoped it wasn't Keith reconsidering. "Hello?"

"Carl!"

"Hello, Trevor." Carl smiled sweetly at his friend's voice.

"I was disappointed you canceled your premiere party, but at least now I know why."

The smile dropped from Carl's face in confusion. "You know why? I told you why. I was too wiped out. The rehearsal schedule is brutal."

"Yeah, huh."

"Why do you think, Trevor?"

"Because you now play a queer!" Trevor laughed. "You think all your old drinking buddies wouldn't torment the crap out of you?"

"Funny, Trev." Carl's skin crawled.

"Man, how did you ever agree to that?"

By the tone in Trevor's voice, Carl could feel the revulsion. "I get paid to act. That's how."

"Did you know they would do that to you when you signed the deal?"

"Actually no. But it's no big deal, Trev."

"No big deal? Sucking face and groping another guy?"

Carl checked his watch, feeling impatient. "Since when are you a homophobe, Trev? I've known you for five years and I've never heard you talk like this."

"Hey, I'm not homophobic. I don't care what people do to each other. I just assumed it would gross you out." After a pause, Trevor asked, "You don't like it, do you?"

"I do what they want me to do. It doesn't matter what I feel personally. It's just my job." Carl felt like screaming in anger at him, but held back.

"What if they ask you to fuck him? Would you?"

"It's not gay porn, Trev. Don't be stupid."

"Would you do gay porn if they asked?"

"I have to get busy on the script. Is this really all you called to talk to me about?"

"No. The guys want to get together again. Maybe shoot some hoops or something. Drink a beer afterwards."

"I'd love to. But it's been very hectic with a tight rehearsal schedule."

"One Sunday afternoon? Come on, Carl. You can't spare a couple of hours?"

The buzzer to his lobby door sounded. Carl crossed the room to hit the entry button for Keith. "Yes. All right."

"Good. This Sunday, meet over at Hugh's place."

"What time?" Carl opened his front door waiting for Keith.

"Eleven?"

"Okay. See you then." He disconnected the call and spotted Keith coming out of the elevator carrying a small backpack.

"Hey."

"Hey." Carl stepped back, allowing Keith to enter and set his bag down. "Everything go all right?"

"I don't know." It came out like a groan of annoyance.

After Carl set the phone back into its cradle, he stood in front of Keith. "Did you break it off?"

"She was at work. It's impossible to have any kind of conversation with her when she's busy."

Carl gestured to the bag. "But you're here and spending the night."

"I am." Keith wrapped around him.

Carl received his kiss. "I suppose that's all that matters."

"It is. Don't worry. I just need to find her a new roommate."

"How are you going to do that?" Carl released him and walked to the kitchen.

"Place an ad in the paper. That's how she found me."

"You want a drink?"

"Sure."

"There're still some leftovers from yesterday. I forgot to bring them into work. You hungry?"

"I'll eat a little."

"Get the script. Read it to me while I set out the food."

Keith was about to get his copy out of his backpack when he noticed Carl's. Picking it up, he sat down at the kitchen table with it. "Have you had a chance to read it?"

"Not all the way through."

Keith flipped pages as Carl placed the leftovers on the table.

"Right." Keith exhaled and read, "Dennis and Troy's

bedroom after dinner. Let's see…we kiss. Okay."

Carl licked a drop of mayonnaise off his finger after he set down the crab salad. Opening a package of sesame crackers, he made up a few topped with the salad, placing them on a plate.

"Take off our shirts…lots of touching and feeling…" Keith continued, "…what!"

"What?" Carl paused, looking down at him.

"How on earth can she get away with this?"

"With what?" Carl walked behind him and leaned over his shoulder.

Keith pointed at the page. "We're both totally nude."

"And?"

"And?" Keith choked in awe. "Like that's not enough?"

"What are we doing?" Carl nudged Keith's hand to open the page farther.

"Simulating intercourse!" Keith shouted. "Look! See the fucking notes?"

"Side shot." Carl pointed it out.

"You don't think you'll be able to see our hard dicks from the side?"

"Hopefully not!" Carl laughed, resuming his job of putting a dollop of crab salad on each cracker.

"Shit. Everyone will know we're hot for each other."

"Keith, relax." Carl set the plate in front of him. Keith grabbed one and stuffed the whole cracker into his mouth. After pouring them both a glass of white zinfandel, Carl dropped onto the chair next to him. "Charlotte will film it in quick little snippets that show lots of back and sides." He smiled at the pun. "And backsides…I wish you remembered her last S and M series better. You'd know her style."

"I'm not talking about the final cut. I'm talking about the gawking crew." Keith picked up another canapé.

"Who the hell gives a shit about them?" Carl sipped his wine. "They just do their job. I bet half of them have wood watching us."

As he shoved more crab salad into his mouth, Keith cracked a smile.

"I'm serious." Carl picked one up to nibble. "For the cameramen and crew its free porn. No, I take that back, they get paid to watch porn."

"Porn." Keith laughed, licking his finger. "Would you ever

do a porn movie?"

"Do it only if you want your mainstream career ended." Carl chewed and swallowed. "I wouldn't want to get anything I did in the bedroom on tape and have it exposed on the net. Male or female."

"No. I suppose not." Keith looked back at the script. "I can't get over these scenes."

"Good thing they don't gross you out." Trevor's words rang in Carl's ears.

Keith ate another cracker and replied, "Funny thing is, it would have if it was someone other than you."

"You don't know that." Carl was extremely flattered.

"I do!" Keith nodded to emphasize it. "You kidding me? Can you imagine having to kiss Marty?" Keith grimaced at the mention of the older character playing Carl's father.

"What about Omar?" Carl asked mischievously.

"Oh? Do you have a thing for him?"

"I don't have a thing." Carl wiped his hands on a napkin. "But he's pretty damn fantastic. That mocha skin? His black hair and dark eyes?"

"Hey! Are you trying to get me jealous again?"

"No. Come on. You can't tell me you don't think Omar is a hunk." Seeing Keith's shy smile, Carl already knew. "Funny how when you've had a gay experience, men suddenly become more attractive."

"To look at," Keith warned.

"To look at." Carl crossed his fingers over his heart. "Promise."

Keith leaned his elbows on the table and gave Carl that grin. That hungry leer he loved so much. It instantly excited Carl. Placing his wine glass on the table, Carl went for a kiss.

Closing his eyes, Carl's fire was lit instantly. Though he'd imagined them reading from the script to begin memorizing their dialogue, he wondered if that would have to wait.

Parting from the kiss, Carl sat back to stare. Keith's hand was rubbing between his own legs. Seeing pure lust in Keith's expression, Carl actually imagined getting on his knees and sucking Keith's cock.

"Uh, you want to fool around first?" Keith opened the top button of his own jeans.

It was so sexy it sent Carl's pulse racing. Moving to sit on

Keith's lap, straddling his legs around Keith, Carl cupped his jaw and devoured his mouth. Digging his hands into Keith's soft hair, Carl groaned in longing as Keith popped the button of Carl's jeans as well.

Deepening their kiss, Carl pushed Keith's head from behind as Keith slid his hand under Carl's shirt, untucking it from his jeans.

While Keith toyed with his nipples, Carl felt the heat rise up in him quickly. It amazed him how excited Keith made him. His touch, his scent, the feel of his tongue and the tiny whimpering moans that filled the room when they connected.

Carl kept asking himself if he could suck Keith. He wanted to. The urge was there. It was the reality he was worried about.

"I want us to go to the bedroom," Keith breathed between kisses.

"Okay." Carl tried to catch his breath. Climbing off Keith's lap, Carl wiped his mouth with the back of his hand, staring at Keith's body, his bulging crotch, and the way the tight jeans curved over his ass as he walked.

When Keith had made it to the threshold of the room, he turned back, reaching out his hand. It was subtle and so sexy, Carl was about to combust. Clasping it, Carl was led to his own bed. Keith released his hand to unzip Carl's jeans. When Keith peeled open Carl's pants, Carl held his breath.

Would Keith suck him?

"Get naked."

Nodding, Carl stepped back and undressed, keeping his eyes on Keith as he did the same.

Once they were both nude, Carl stood still, waiting.

Keith closed in on him, embracing him, finding his lips again. Wrapping around him, Carl sealed their bodies together, relishing the heat of Keith's flesh on his. Running his hands down Keith's silky sides, Carl began inching his way between them, rubbing the backs of his hands against Keith's abdomen. Keith's hips parted from his just enough to give Carl access.

As he lowered his hands, Carl felt his own cock and Keith's. Instinctively he enveloped them both, pressing them together in his palms.

Keith paused from the kiss to release a deep, passionate groan of pleasure.

Staring down at their two cocks nestled together, Carl licked his lips in desire. He wanted to see what Keith's cock tasted like. Would it taste the same as the rest of Keith's skin?

"Go lie down." Carl released his hold on them.

Stumbling backward, Keith found the bed and lay back on it.

Psyching himself up, Carl's internal dialogue kept babbling. If it isn't nice to suck Keith, would it look odd if I pulled away? If I like it, will I be able to take Keith coming in my mouth? Swallow? Would Keith be patient and let me try and give him a blowjob? Experiment?

Carl stared down at Keith's entire body as he lay prone on the bed. The look of anticipation on Keith's face was amazing. Should I ask him if it's okay? Or just do it?

Inhaling deeply, Carl climbed on the bed from the foot, crawling his way up to Keith.

Keith spread his legs wide, as if begging for it.

Lowering down to his elbows between Keith's knees, Carl caught Keith propping his head up on a pillow to watch.

Will I get a case of stage fright? Or should I just dive in?

Carl decided to ease into it slowly, since it was obvious Keith was very keen on the idea.

Closing his eyes, Carl kissed the smooth skin on the inside of Keith's thighs. Keith's leg muscles tightened and he whimpered softly. Raising his head, Carl stared at Keith's balls and long, erect shaft. The scent of male testosterone made his skin tingle. Carl closed his eyes again and nestled against Keith's heavy sack. As he did, Keith's testicles tightened up, moving against Carl's closed lips. Carl rubbed them gently with his mouth and jaw, enjoying Keith's reactions of bliss.

Scooting higher, Carl touched the long, silky length of Keith's dick. It bobbed and seeped in response.

"Oh, God..." Keith moaned softly.

Licking his dry lips, Carl touched his closed mouth against Keith's cock. It felt hot and throbbed when he did. Running his lips from the base to under the corona, Carl heard Keith whimpering in agony.

He wanted to suck it. Face it, Carl, you're dying to do this.

Climbing even higher on Keith's body, Carl aimed Keith's seeping head at his mouth. After glancing up at Keith whose rapt attention and tight posture were clenched in anticipation, Carl opened his lips. Very slowly, he used his tongue to touch the skin of the head of Keith's cock.

A low, agonized moan erupted from Keith.

It tasted like the rest of Keith's body. Slightly salty and clean. As he grew bolder the tip of his tongue dragged across the slit. Closing his mouth, Carl registered the taste of his pre-come drop for a moment. It certainly wasn't repugnant.

Keith's hands clenched the bedspread in white knuckles.

Using his fingers to aim Keith's cock to his mouth, Carl opened his lips and allowed the head to enter. Keith's hips jerked up almost in reflex to penetrate and more stickiness oozed out. Carl knew Keith was so keyed up, that the possibility of his shooting his wad was getting very real. "Warn me."

"Yes," Keith replied from a strangled throat.

At least now Carl felt like he had the option of rejecting it. Closing his eyes, trying to relax his body, which was almost as tight as Keith's at the moment, Carl lowered once again to take just the head into his mouth. With his tongue he explored it, registering the tightness of the skin and the width of it as he closed his lips over it completely.

Again Keith's hips rose up, craving deeper penetration. Carl knew it, but wanted to take it slowly. He had no idea what it would feel like to have his entire mouth filled with a man's dick.

Backing off, catching his breath, Carl stroked Keith gently, realizing the time this was taking must be excruciating for Keith. Once again, closing his eyes, Carl opened his lips. This time he pushed it in a little deeper. Keith almost howled in agony. "Fuck!"

"I'm sorry. Do you want me to stop?" Carl asked.

"No! Are you kidding me?" came his breathless reply.

Amazed this slow torture was exciting Keith as much as it was him, Carl continued. Pushing Keith's cock towards him, Carl opened wide and tried to fit it halfway in. Very gently, he allowed it to glide back out. Keith was going wild, vocalizing every tormenting move.

Carl had finally come to the conclusion that it wasn't bad. He had sucked Keith's fingers like they were a cock. Okay, this wasn't his finger, but in reality, Keith's body had already penetrated him in so many ways, this was just one more. It was swallowing Carl was worried about. He felt like he had the rest down pretty well.

Getting to his knees for a better angle, Carl held Keith's dick between his index finger and thumb, and began moving up and down on it with his mouth, sucking hard as he did.

The moment he allowed Keith complete penetration, Carl heard him shout, "I'm there!"

Carl jerked back and tilted Keith's cock away from him. It spurted creamy come all over Keith's abdomen.

"Sorry," Carl whispered. "I just didn't know if I was ready for that."

"Sorry?" Keith gasped in amazement. "It was fantastic!"

"Was it? I feel like such a fucking amateur." Carl climbed off the bed to get a tissue.

"Just having it in your mouth, Carl, was unbelievable."

Carl returned, wiping the spill from Keith's body.

"Thanks."

"No problem." Carl set the tissue on the nightstand and lay next to him.

Keith wondered what Carl expected from him. Rolling to his side, propping up his head, Keith asked, "What do you want me to do?"

"What are you comfortable doing?" Carl ran his hand along Keith's side.

Keith didn't think he was ready to give Carl a blowjob. At least he didn't think he was. "You want to fuck me?"

"Yeah?" Carl seemed surprised.

"Well, it felt pretty good when you used your finger."

"Don't do it if you don't feel ready, Keith."

"What's to do? I just lay here, right?"

"Don't trivialize it."

"I'm not. Are you kidding? Do you know what it means to me that you went down on me?" Keith dug his hand through Carl's dark hair.

"I love you. I want to please you."

"Did you hate it?"

"No. Not at all. I think with time, I could even swallow."

Keith lowered his hands down Carl's body, dragging his fingers over his hard protruding cock. "Fuck me."

Carl gripped Keith's jaw. "Are you sure?" he enunciated slowly.

"Yes." Keith felt his stomach tighten but he wanted to try it.

Carl kissed him, urging Keith to his back, connecting their chests together.

Loving that kiss, the way it communicated Carl's love and attraction to him, Keith felt his body respond and grow hard again.

After a long bout of kissing and caressing, Carl sat back reaching into the nightstand.

Keith felt as if he were holding his breath. *If I hate it, he'll stop. No big deal.*

Forcing himself to quit panting as Carl slid a condom on and coated it with the gel, Keith tried not to panic or back out. After all, Carl had sucked him.

"Okay, babe?"

"Okay." Keith was hyperventilating.

Carl crawled down the bed, gently parting Keith's thighs. His chest rising and falling like a bellows, Keith allowed Carl to place each one of his legs on Carl's shoulders, offering a clear path to his ass.

As Keith looked on, Carl squeezed more lube on his fingers.

The first cool touch to his back passage, Keith flinched.

"You okay?"

"Yes." Keith tucked his arms under his back, bracing himself.

Very tenderly, Carl penetrated him, smoothing his slick fingers in and out.

Instantly the pleasure sparked through him. "God, that's amazing!"

Carl chuckled softly. "Good."

The strength of the rush it sent through him confirmed Keith's determination to do this act. It felt absolutely incredible being entered that way.

When Carl got to his knees and placed the head of his cock on Keith's ass, he whispered, "I love you."

It brought a lump to Keith's throat. "I love you too."

"Thank you for sharing your body this way, Keith."

A hot tear raced down Keith's face. "I want to. So much."

At that comment, Carl pushed in.

Keith gasped and arched his back. Carl's size filled him. As his brain tried to reconcile the act, Keith wondered if this was what a woman felt like. Receiving. Receiving the penetration, the filling of her body for her man. *Christ! I'm a fucking woman!*

But the voice in Keith's head wasn't criticizing him, it was acknowledging what the other half felt like. And it didn't feel bad. It was fulfilling. Made him feel whole. Two becoming one.

Through his gasps, Carl asked, "You okay?"

"Yes!" Keith felt intense sparks of pleasure he just couldn't ignore. Releasing his hands he grabbed his own cock and began jerking it off.

"Oh, baby!" Carl lit up and began thrusting in earnest.

Taking it up to the root, Keith felt like passing out from the strength of the heat and excitement. Hearing Carl's heavy breathing and grunting, seeing his face fill with orgasmic passion, the sensation of being entered, consumed, Keith had never felt anything like it in his life. It was paradise. Rapture on the grandest scale.

As his balls churned and gave up their contents, and it surged out of his cock, Keith could not prevent his expletives of emotion from pouring out of his mouth. "Aaaaugh Holy-mother-fucking-God!" As Carl thrust deep and hard, Keith came, shooting come past his face to the pillow behind him. Blinking in shock, he focused in on Carl and could not believe what he looked like. Ecstasy washed across his handsome features as he came. His expression was a cross between angelic and demonic. "Carl! Carl!" Keith panted, wanting to shout out his epiphany of discovery to him. I like being gay!

"Holy shit..." Carl groaned, his body drooping from the exhaustion.

Wanting to hold him, embrace him, Keith waited for Carl to pull out. "Oh, Carl..." Keith milked his cock as he moaned, feeling the waves subside slowly.

Slowly coming to reality, Carl set Keith's legs back on the bed, pulling out, holding the edge of the rubber.

The moment he was released, Keith knelt up and wrapped around Carl, hugging him.

"Oh, my beautiful lover," Carl crooned, squeezing him tight. "That was un-fucking-real."

A rush of emotion slapped Keith senseless. The depth of adoration he felt for Carl engulfed him. This must be real love. There's no other explanation for it.

Unable to prevent it, a sob escaped Keith's lips.

Instantly Carl backed up, panic-stricken, to see his face.

Shaking his head, Keith tried to speak. "No. I'm fine. I'm just overwhelmed."

Exhaling in relief, Carl kissed him gently.

"I love you," Keith began to cry as he spoke those magical

words. "I can't believe how much I love you."

"Oh, sugar," Carl melted, crushing Keith in his embraced. "I love, love, love you."

Gaining some control, Keith asked with a jerky breath, "How did this happen? How did we do this?"

"I don't know. Is there any rhyme or reason to true happiness? To true love?" Carl dabbed at Keith's tears.

Keith fought to control his sobs. Carl climbed off the bed, helping Keith stand so they could wash up.

"We need to learn our lines," Carl laughed as if that idea was almost impossible.

"I know." Keith washed his face, and body quickly. "I think my come hit your pillow."

Carl caught Keith's eye in the mirror. "You're joking."

"No." Keith laughed.

Immediately Carl left the bathroom returning with the pillow. "Look at this!" he shouted proudly. "If that ain't real pleasure, what is?"

Keith broke up with laughter as Carl removed the soiled case. "You made me come so hard, I almost hurt myself!"

Carl doubled over with hilarity.

Keith kept dabbing at his eyes as they filled from the his joy.

"Oh, Keith. I love you, you know that?" Carl tossed the case in the laundry, finding a replacement.

"Right. Back to work." Keith felt groggy and lightheaded.

"Yes. Funny." Carl tossed the pillow back on the bed. "Back to pretend love scenes."

"God, our life is bizarre."

"No kidding. But it's wonderful though, isn't it?" Carl cupped Keith's face for a kiss.

"Yes. It's like a dream." Keith stared into Carl's green eyes.

"Okay." Carl found his briefs and slipped his jeans back on. "Teach me your trick for memorizing the lines so quickly."

As he zipped his pants, Keith replied, "It's easy."

"Good."

They returned to the living room. While Carl went to get their wine, Keith sat down and relaxed, smiling contentedly at him. Heaven. He'd found heaven.

Chapter Twelve

Keith couldn't put his parents off any longer. He met them for lunch at Literati's on Wilshire Boulevard. Parking his car, he found his dad standing out in front of the main entrance. As he approached Keith tucked his shirt into his jeans and ran his hand over his hair nervously. He had no idea why he was so anxious about seeing him, but he was.

"Hello, Keith."

"Dad." Keith gave him a quick hug and asked, "Mom inside?"

"Yes. She wanted to get a table before it got too crowded."

Keith walked through the busy room and noticed his mother waving to him from a table near the wall of windows. It was bright and lively inside with the noise of chatting voices and forks touching plates.

"Hi, Mom." Keith leaned over to kiss her cheek.

"Hello, dear. You're looking very well." She smiled proudly at him.

Keith wondered if all the hot sex he was having was making him glow. The thought made him smile wryly. He took a seat across from his mother, as his father sat next to her, their backs facing the view outside.

Once he had relaxed and set his napkin on his lap Keith picked up one of the menus. "Did you already decide?"

"I did, but your father hasn't had a chance."

"What are you getting, Sandy?" Ron asked.

"I was just thinking of ordering the wood-grilled burger."

Keith set his menu down. "Sounds good to me."

"So, Keith," Sandy wriggled in excitement, "how does it feel to be a big star?"

"I'm not exactly a big star yet, Mom." Keith took a quick look around to make sure no one was eavesdropping.

"You will be. Just be patient."

The waiter approached their table. "Are you ready to order?"

After they gave him their selections and the waiter left, Keith picked up his glass of ice water and noticed his dad's expression seemed pinched. "Everything okay at work, Dad?"

"Hm? Oh. Yes. Work is fine."

Sandy nudged Ron in what appeared to Keith as admonishment. Keith asked, "What's going on?" A sudden cold ball filled Keith's belly.

His parents exchanged pained looks.

Keith knew. He didn't have to ask. "Dad…it's acting."

"How can they make you do things like that to another man?" Keith was surprised at how angry he sounded. "It's disgusting," Ron continued, "Did you know they would make you do that when you took the offer?"

"Ron, calm down." Sandy grabbed his arm.

"Yes, my agent warned me."

"And you took the job anyway?" Ron choked in amazement.

"I need to work, Dad. Adam has been trying to get me a decent part for months. I wasn't interested in waiting tables like Patty does, believe me."

"It's sick. I can't even watch the show any longer. You, kissing that man."

Keith wondered what his father would do it he knew they were doing far more than that both on the show and in reality.

"Ron," Sandy spoke up, "it's just a silly acting job. Why are you getting so upset about it? I'm proud of Keith. He's working in a number one television series. I don't see why you can't see the difference between acting and real life."

"He still has to touch a man, Sandy." Ron gulped his water as if it were vodka.

"Isn't that my problem?" Keith asked. He had no idea his father was a homophobe. It simply had never come up before in the household. Since he had been straight, and his sister dated men, Keith didn't remember ever discussing the issue of gay relationships with either of his parents. This was a rude awakening. Keith was not pleased with his father's attitude about it. "Besides, Dad, what's the big deal? Since when do you have a problem with gay men?"

"I don't have a problem with gay men," he snapped. "I have a problem watching my own son kiss a man."

The rage in him growing, Keith asked boldly, "Oh? So if I were gay you'd hate me?"

Sandy intervened. "You're not. So why are we discussing this? Change the topic."

Ron pointed a warning finger at Keith, "Don't even think about it."

Keith let out a sarcastic laugh. "Don't think about it?"

"Please, can we change the subject?" Sandy pleaded.

"No." Keith sat up taller in the chair. "We can't." Addressing his father, Keith said, "What if I told you I was gay, Dad? Huh? What would you do? Disown me? Punch me?"

"Keith, why are you antagonizing your father?"

Staring at his dad's steel blue eyes, seeing a side of him he never had before, Keith finally understood the depth of prejudice gay men, or for that matter, any minority, faced. It was a rude awakening. "I cannot believe I am hearing this from my own father."

"And I don't understand why you are making this an issue," Ron replied.

Grinding his jaw, Keith leaned over the table towards him. "Because I like touching Carl."

"Keith!" Sandy scolded. "Stop this. Behave."

"You know what, Dad?" Keith's words were dipped in spite. "I always admired you. I thought you were awesome in so many ways. But now? I think you're an ignorant pig." Keith threw his napkin on the table.

"Keith!" Sandy chided. "What on earth has come over you? This is so unlike you."

"What's come over me is the realization that love is never wrong. It doesn't matter who the hell you love. And the fact that people do love each other shouldn't fucking matter to anyone else. It's no one's fucking business but their own. You get that, Dad?" Keith stood. "I can't sit here anymore."

"Keith," Sandy implored, "please stay."

"No. See ya, Mom." He turned his back on them and left the restaurant. "Son of a bitch," Keith mumbled as he unlocked his car. "I had no idea you were a fucking asshole, Dad."

Carl stuck his sunglasses on as he stepped out of his car. He walked to the front door of Hugh's home and rang the bell.

The door opened and Hugh shouted, "Carl! Come inside."

"Hey, Hugh." He stepped into the cool interior and found everyone lounging in living room drinking beer.

"Carl!" Trevor shouted as the other three men waved their greeting.

"Want a beer?" Hugh asked.

"Sure." Carl moved his sunglasses to the top of his head. "Hey, guys. How you all doing?"

"You ready for a game in the heat?" John asked, his legs straddled, his long army print shorts almost covering his knees.

"As long as we can jump in the pool after," Carl replied, laughing. When Hugh returned with his beer, Carl took it, sipping it. "Thanks."

"My pleasure." Hugh picked up his own beer from the coffee table.

"How are we split up?" Carl asked.

Trevor pointed, "You, me and Bob, against Hugh, John, and Dick."

"Ouch!" Carl laughed, "Who the hell decided that? We'll slaughter you."

"Yeah, right," John shook his head. "We'll see about that."

"What are we waiting for," Carl asked, "the fucking afternoon heat?"

"We were waiting for you. Let's go." Hugh signaled.

As he followed Hugh out of the back of the house, Carl drank another gulp of his beer, setting it down in the kitchen as they passed through it to the backyard.

Slipping his sunglasses back onto his nose, Carl admired the large, finely trimmed garden, built-in pool, tennis courts, and the basketball court. Even though it was only eleven, the heat was already noticeable.

While they waited for Hugh to get the basketball out of a large storage shed, Dick leaned against Carl and asked, "Why did they turn your character gay? That must suck."

Knowing it was only a matter of time before he got teased by these men, Carl told himself he would laugh it off and not take it personally. "Yeah. It does suck. But that's life."

John overheard and walked over. "I wasn't going to bring it up. But since Dick has, how the fuck do you do it?"

As the crowd of men gathered around him suddenly, Carl felt like he was a victim of the inquisition. "It's acting. I do my job and go home."

"Do they make you guys do more than just kiss?" Trevor asked, his nose curling in disgust.

"Yes. Unfortunately." Carl tried to keep calm. The last thing he wanted was to be outed in front of his macho drinking buddies.

"Sick!" Bob cringed. "Like what?"

"You don't want the gory details." Carl looked over their shoulders trying to hurry Hugh up. It seemed he'd been delayed and was crouching down pumping the ball up with air.

"Please tell me you don't have to touch the guy's cock." Trevor winced in revulsion.

"Fuck no. It's just a cable drama, not porno, you idiot."

"How far do they make you go?" John asked.

"It's all just hype. They just make it look like we're really doing things."

"Yes, but you actually had to kiss him." Dick's intense stare was unnerving.

"I just close my eyes and pretend it's Cheryl Jones."

"Now, she's hot!" Trevor exhaled.

"Have you asked her out, Carl?" John nudged him.

"She's going out with someone already." Carl watched Hugh bounce the ball, finally coming their way.

"Okay, men!" Hugh shouted. "Let's play!"

Hoping that was an end to the topic, Carl engrossed himself in a game of hot, sweaty basketball.

Keith checked his watch as he climbed the stairs to his apartment. Patty was home, sitting on the outside deck reading a magazine. After he tossed his keys on the counter he opened the sliding screen door. "Hey."

"You're back early."

"I know."

"Let me guess. Your dad and you had a fight about the gay character."

Keith pulled the second plastic chair around to straddle backwards, resting his head on his arms as they lay on the seatback. "Yes."

"Well, you had a feeling."

"I don't get it, Patty. It's just a stupid acting job. What's it to

161

him?"

She flipped the glossy pages as she replied, "It's embarrassing for a dad to see his son kiss a guy. Period."

"I suppose." Keith sighed and lay his head down on his arms, closing his eyes. "Anyone answer the ad yet?"

"Nope."

"Well, it's only been in the paper one day."

"Where are you going to live?"

"I don't know." He wanted to move in with Carl.

"You can't move back home now."

"I never wanted to move back home." Keith felt the warmth of the sun on his skin and it made him want to sleep.

"Keith."

He forced himself to raise his head to meet her eyes, though he was very comfortable with his head down. "What?"

"Why don't you just tell me you've met someone else?"

"Because that's not the reason why I'm moving."

"Then what is?"

"I just need my own space."

"You could just stay in the spare bedroom. I won't bother you."

"I know. But think how awkward it'll be when you start bringing other guys home." He smiled sadly. "I'll get jealous."

"Do you know how expensive apartments are? Have you looked?"

"I have." He dropped his head back down and closed his eyes again.

"Big spender suddenly? Are you rolling in money?"

"Hardly. But I think I can afford a studio apartment somewhere." He was looking for something within walking distance to Carl's condo with a little luck.

"Was it weird having to kiss a guy?"

Keith inhaled deeply wondering if he was going to get asked that question eternally. "Yes. But I'm getting used to it."

"That Carl Bronson is so damn good looking. At least you're kissing a hunk and not some ugly fucker."

"I suppose." Keith wondered how long Carl was going to be playing basketball. He wanted to snuggle up with him for a nap…after some hot sex.

"Is he a good kisser?"

Smiling to himself, Keith knew what he wanted to say. He

162

just didn't think it was wise. Sitting up again to see her expression, Keith found she was fascinated with the topic. "Do you get off on two guys kissing?"

"A little. It was pretty hot watching you two in the premiere episode."

He chuckled softly. "Amazing. I had no idea women liked that."

"Why? Guys get all horny about two women."

"True." He stood and moved the plastic chair aside. "I have to take a nap. I'm wiped out."

"It's the heat."

"Probably." He waved and walked to the spare room. After he kicked off his shoes he stretched out and yawned. Finding his mobile phone, he dialed it and held it to his ear.

"Hello?"

"Hey. You still at your friend's place?"

"Yes. Hang on."

Keith waited for a moment. Listening intently.

"You there?" Carl asked.

"Yes."

"I just wanted some privacy. Where are you?"

"Home. I was about to take a nap and I got horny thinking about you."

"Well, to be honest, I was about to head home. We played for about an hour and a half, and now we're all just hanging around Hugh's pool. I'm exhausted."

"Are we getting together later?"

"If you want, you can meet me at my place in about an hour."

"Oh! Cool." Keith sat up.

"See ya then?"

"Am I staying overnight?" Keith wanted to.

"Sure."

Smiling excitedly, Keith replied, "See you soon."

"See ya."

Keith hung up, hopping off the bed, feeling more motivated than he had a minute ago. As he found some clothing to take with him, Patty stepped into the room.

"You're packing your backpack? I thought you were taking a nap."

Keith froze. "Uh."

"Keith, just tell me you're dating someone else. What's the

big deal? We're not exactly a couple anymore."

Turning to face her, Keith hated the idea that anything he did could hurt her. "I'm just staying at Carl's place. We practice learning our lines until late, and I end up crashing in his spare room."

"Oh?" She narrowed her eyes at him suspiciously.

He avoided looking at her. "So...I'll see you sometime tomorrow night after your shift."

"You think it looks good? You sleeping with the guy?"

"We're not sleeping together so don't say stupid things." Keith felt a sick sensation creep into his stomach as he continued to gather what he needed.

"It still looks like you are."

"Now you sound like my dad. Cut it out, Patty." He glared at her and tried not to worry.

Carl disconnected the call and dropped the phone into his shorts' pocket. Walking back to the pool where the rest of the group was splayed out on chaise lounge chairs, he looked down at them.

Hugh shielded his eyes from the glare and asked, "Everything okay, Carl?"

"Yes. But I was thinking of calling it a day, boys."

A rumble of protests surrounded him.

"We were going to have a barbeque for dinner," Trevor announced. "Where do you have to go?"

"I've got to learn the new script. It's a very tight schedule. I only have a few days between each shooting."

"Ahh, the glamorous world of an actor." John rolled his eyes. "Kissing a man for a living."

"Come on. Cut me some slack, John." Carl took his car keys out of his pocket.

"Yeah, John," Dick replied. "Don't rub it in. Pity the poor schmuck."

Carl hid his cringe at the comment. No one should pity him for kissing Keith O'Leary. Not by a long shot. "Right. Thanks for including me in the game. I appreciate it."

Trevor hopped off the lounge chair. "I'll walk you out."

Carl waved, "See ya!" to the rest of the men and slid back the sliding door to walk through the house to the front door. Just as he stepped outside, Carl felt Trevor's hand on his shoulder. He peered back at him to say goodbye. "See you soon?"

Trevor smiled at him, holding out his hand for a shake. "Yes. We'll most likely get together for a beer next weekend."

"I'll try, but I can't make any promises until the season ends." Feeling the grip on his hand tighten instead of release, Carl studied Trevor's eyes curiously. "What?"

"You sure you can handle all the crap you're going to be hit with?"

"Crap? What crap?" Carl took back his hand.

"The tabloids. I read in that weekly rag at the check-out line that you and the dude who plays Dennis are a couple."

Carl felt his blood go cold. Keeping his exterior composure, Carl sighed, "Well, don't believe any of the shit you read in those things."

"I don't. I just feel really bad you have to be labeled like that. It's not fair, Carl."

"I'll survive. Besides, the producers will love the publicity."

"I'm surprised you're taking this so well."

"What am I supposed to do? Shoot myself?"

"I'd hitch up with a girlfriend if I were you and get yourself seen in public. You don't need that fucking stereotype, do you?"

Shifting his body weight uncomfortably, Carl answered, "To be honest, Trevor, I don't give a fuck. I won't be the first actor to be put through it in the press. You just have to ignore it."

"All right, buddy. Just giving you the heads up."

"I appreciate it, Trev. But don't worry. I let that shit roll off my back."

"Right. So, see you soon?"

"You will." Carl waved and continued his walk to his car with a heavy heart.

Keith sat in his car waiting. Finally seeing the Corvette pulling up to the gate, Keith grabbed his backpack, got out and pocketed his key as he walked past the gate to meet Carl.

Standing back as Carl parked in his garage and used a remote to close the door, he approached him and noticed Carl had a newspaper tucked under his arm. "Hi, Carl."

"Hey." Carl handed him the paper. "It's already started."

"What has?" Keith took the newspaper and found it was

folded to a specific page. As Carl unlocked the door to the lobby, Keith read the headline. "Forever Young's Newest Gay Couple an Overnight Sensation."

Once they were standing in the elevator together, Keith asked, "So? What's it say? Give me the gist of it."

"It's mostly about us as the characters, not as real people. But there is some slight innuendo that we may be attached outside work."

"Should I not be staying over?" Keith handed him back the paper.

Carl shrugged. "I don't fucking know."

Once Carl had opened the door and they were inside his condo, Keith set his pack down by the door, in case he wasn't staying.

"I have to shower."

"Okay." Following Carl as he headed to the bedroom to strip, Keith picked up the newspaper Carl had set it down on the kitchen table. Reading it as he loitered in the bedroom with him, Keith scanned the article quickly. "It doesn't say we're together outside the show. Where does it say that?"

Carl stood beside him and read through the print.

Realizing he was naked, Keith caressed Carl's low back, running his hand over his tight ass.

"Here. Just one line. It says, 'The two actors have shown instant chemistry and animal attraction giving their sex scenes a touch of realism.'"

"That doesn't mean shit." Keith released his hold on the newspaper and stood behind Carl admiring him and touching his silky warm skin. Wrapping around him from behind, Keith squeezed him close, sniffing at his neck and hair. "You always smell so good."

"I do? I'm filthy. I was playing basketball."

"I know. I even like your sweat scent." Keith stuck his nose in Carl's armpit.

Carl dropped the paper and reached behind him to touch Keith.

Pressing his face against Carl's back, Keith cupped Carl's pectoral muscles and pressed his hard cock against Keith's ass.

"Why don't you take off your clothing?" Carl purred.

"Why don't I?" Keith agreed. After another deep inhale of Carl's body, Keith parted from him to undress.

Hopping to yank off his jeans, Keith was naked quickly and wrapped around Carl again, facing him. Breathing in Carl's masculine scent was an intense aphrodisiac to Keith. It sent his cock upright and throbbing. "Christ, I can't get enough of you."

Carl laughed softly. "You sure you don't want me to shower first?"

"No." Keith licked his chest, groaning in delight at the saltiness. Lapping Carl's taut skin, Keith ran his tongue downwards until he was kneeling before him.

With Carl's erect prick in front of his face, Keith stroked it gently, admiring it. Tasting the salt of Carl's skin on his lips, Keith became hungry for him. He wanted to try oral sex.

"Keith?"

"Yes?" Keith raised his chin to see Carl's face.

"Can I lie down? I'm pretty wiped out."

"Of course." The pause gave Keith some time to get psyched up for it.

Watching Carl move was intoxicating. Keith thought he was catlike in his gestures. Perhaps Carl had some dance training. Keith never thought to ask him before.

Gazing longingly at Carl as he fell into a naturally relaxed pose on the bed, Keith felt his mouth watering in anticipation.

"I'm ready now, babe." Carl reached out.

Keith leaned over and kissed Carl's shin lightly. Running a line of kisses up Carl's massive thigh muscle, Keith felt his own cock pulsating in excitement. Everything he and Carl did was new, an exploration of the most amazing kind. Keith never experienced foreplay as good as this before. Trying not to get wrapped up in his thoughts, Keith knew it was because of the amount he loved Carl that this was so enticing.

He wanted to please him. And by pleasing Carl, he was ultimately pleasing himself.

As Keith approached Carl's crotch, Carl spread his legs so Keith could crawl between them.

Kneeling, a hand on each thigh, Keith kissed Carl's balls lightly. "Damn you smell incredible."

Carl sighed deeply in reply, his hands behind his head, propping him up so he could watch Keith.

Staring at Carl's long shaft, at its blushing color and engorged veins, Keith was fascinated by it. With the back of his hand he stroked its tight satiny skin. It bobbed in response. Keith moved closer, so his knee was pressed tightly against Carl's balls. Leaning over, Keith used his right hand to bring Carl's cock upright. Aiming Carl's cock at his mouth, Keith closed his eyes and decided to just try sucking it.

Feeling Carl's round, mushroom-shaped head brush past his lips, Keith shivered at the thrill, knowing how this must feel to Carl.

Carl groaned a deep rumbling sound and tensed his muscles.

Keith allowed Carl's cock further into his mouth and drew his lips down on it. Feeling it pulsate and move caused the chills to wash over Keith's body. He sucked it strongly and tasted a salty drop on his tongue. It wasn't horrible. And certainly didn't make him withdraw and change his mind. But of course, knowing what may happen, Keith allowed Carl's cock to slip out of his lips and whispered, "Tell me if you're going to come."

"I will. It feels incredible, Keith. Thank you."

Adjusting his body to a more comfortable position, Keith stretched out his legs so he could press his own cock into the bed and relaxed both elbows on Carl's thighs. Directing Carl's penis towards him again, Keith slid him back in, deeper this time, tightening his lips around it, loving the way it vibrated on his tongue. Pausing to savor the sensation of it filling him, the way it had when he was taken anally, Keith moaned in pleasure and felt Carl tense up and tilt his hips higher.

Drawing it out of his mouth again, sucking as hard as he could, Keith heard Carl's whimper and knew damn well it was too slow to make him come. Leaning up higher for better leverage, Keith glided it into his mouth more quickly, raising and lowering his head as he did, each time trying to fit more of it into his mouth. At one point Keith's lips made it to the base of Carl's cock. Carl gasped and reached for Keith's hair, massaging his scalp, encouraging him.

Keith couldn't believe how much he was enjoying it. He actually liked it better than going down on a female for the reason that he knew Carl was not faking it. He never trusted a woman once he found out that they did on occasion.

"Oh, Keith...that is amazing."

Hearing Carl's satisfying declarations, Keith imagined the surprise and delight in Carl if he could swallow. Could he? Would he gag? Would it cause him to choke and ruin the mood? Keith had no idea.

Assuming he would do what Carl had done, removing it from his mouth to allow him to ejaculate outside, Keith just wasn't sure what he would do. A month ago Keith couldn't even imagine kissing a man, and that soon changed. It was a dare. Keith was daring himself to do it just for the thrill of Carl's reaction.

But first he had to get him there.

Taking a break to relax his jaw, Keith caught his breath and stroked Carl a few times in his hand. Forming a strategy in his head, Keith shifted to the side and began rubbing Carl's balls and between his legs near his ass.

Carl hissed out a tight breath and his hips elevated off the bed. Right. Do that and suck. Keith gripped the base of Carl's cock and began sucking with a purpose. Moving as quickly as he could up and down, drawing with strong pulls of his mouth, all the while pressing his fingers up against Carl's ass, Keith heard his warning.

"Agh! Keith! I'm going to come."

Keith closed his eyes tighter and kept it up.

"Keith! Ah! Keith! I can't hold it!"

The whimpering moans stoked the fire in Keith. His own cock was so hard it was dying for release. He felt like yelling, "Come!" But he didn't want to stop.

A choking grunt came from Carl as his body jerked back.

Keith prepared himself for a cosmic blast. He felt it first through a rapid pulsating against the finger which was pressing into Carl's ass. Instantly Carl's cock fluttered, throbbing like mad. And the come hit Keith's mouth like a fountain of spray. Shocked at the force, Keith held it in his mouth and knew he had to swallow or spit it out. He swallowed.

Sitting back, trying to catch his breath and relax his jaw muscles, Keith absorbed silently what he had just done.

Before he could digest it, Carl dove on him, smacking him back so hard he almost fell off the bed.

"Oh my fucking God!" Carl gasped, gulping the air. "You fantastic mother fucker! I love you! I love you!"

Laughing as Carl covered him with kisses all over his face, Keith felt so wonderful at that moment he couldn't put it into words.

Carl didn't think Keith would do it. But when he did, it

169

knocked Carl off his feet. Wrapping around Keith, writhing against his body, Carl was so high from it, he was near tears. "I am so in love with you. Christ, Keith, you are beautiful, fantastic!"

"It wasn't that bad."

At the modesty and sweetness Keith was showing, Carl wanted to return the favor. "I'll do it to you. Shall I? Shall I try? I promise I'll swallow. Or do you want my ass? Anything, lover, anything." Licking Keith's neck, chewing on his jaw and earlobe, Carl was already hot for his second climax.

"I want to make love to you."

"Yes. Yes, of course. Oh, Keith, I love you so much." Carl could not get over the fact that Keith had swallowed. No one ever had with him before. He cupped Keith's face tightly in his hands and kissed him, tasting his own come in amazement. Carl went mad on him, sucking at his tongue and grinding his hips against Keith's. He was spinning, delirious, and so excited he could hardly function. Never had he felt love like this. Never. And he was so wild about Keith, he couldn't imagine a life without him.

"Oh, babe, lover…take me. Take me hard. Screw me. Make my body yours."

"Oh, Carl…" Keith choked up, cupping Carl's face tenderly. "The things you say to me amaze me."

"I mean every word." Carl couldn't catch his breath, kissing him again. Carl broke the kiss and rushed to find the rubbers and lube. "Here. How do you want me?"

Breathing hard, sitting up, Keith whispered, "Face me. Please."

"Yes. Anything you want." Carl handed him the rubbers, lying back, bending his knees, spreading his legs wide.

Keith opened the small package and slid the condom on.

Carl was already in heat watching him. Though it sounded silly, Carl kept wanting to repeat how much he loved Keith. It was such a strange craving to want to tell him over and over.

More confidently than before, Keith entered Carl's ass with slippery fingers, rubbing his magic spot like a pro.

Carl shivered and jerked his hips up in response. "Keith! You're getting so fucking good at everything."

"Feel nice?"

"Holy Christ." Carl ground his jaw as the sensation of ecstasy raced over his body. "Aaahh! Fuck me, Keith!"

"My pleasure."

Unable to catch his breath from all the excitement, Carl panted deeply as he watched. His legs were raised to Keith's shoulders, and Keith kissed each of Carl's calves as he did.

Warm pressure followed by penetration filled Carl's body. As Keith eased into him, Carl felt his emotions rise to breaking point. He wanted to please Keith, to feel Keith's body in his. He loved them becoming one in this act of love-making. It was the vital event of their union to confirm how they felt about each other.

"Oh, Carl…"

"I know, baby, I know." Carl clenched his teeth and eyes, tears spilling down his temples. At the flash of intense pleasure, Carl grabbed his own cock and jacked it off. He had to come again, he was going mad.

Keith's thrusting intensified. As Carl felt Keith deepening his penetration and speed, Carl fisted himself faster.

In the throes of an orgasm, Keith moaned, "Carl, oh my God, Carl…"

"Come on, baby…come on…" Carl came to the music of Keith's moans, spurting come over his chest and feeling Keith's length shudder inside him.

After Keith had come, Carl covered his face to hide his tears. He had no idea why he was crying. Then again, maybe he did. He had to hide his love. It became an agonizing pain in his chest. Today, with his friends, lying, pretending he didn't enjoy the contact, it was torture.

Keith recovered slowly. The climax was so intense it felt as if he would black out from the swoon. Pulling out, allowing Carl's legs to settle back on the bed, Keith heard his sob and quickly raised his head to see him. "Oh, God." Keith dropped the spent condom on the floor and crawled up over Carl's body. "What? Did I hurt you? Carl?"

"No. You didn't hurt me."

Collapsing down on top of Carl's body, Keith hugged him. "Please don't cry."

Carl wrapped his arms around Keith and hid his face as he wailed.

"Please! What? Carl!" Keith was so worried he was sick. "What did I do?"

As if he had to force himself to speak, Carl cried, "It's not you. It's having to hide."

"Oh, babe, I understand." Keith snaked his arms around Carl's neck and drew him against him. Feeling Carl's body wracked with sobs under him, Keith's heart broke. "I'm sorry. We have to. Please, Carl."

"I know." He hiccupped and tried to wipe his eyes. After another minute, Carl quieted down. "Today, with the guys. I had to lie. It sucked."

"Believe me. I get it. It was hell with my dad today as well." Keith moved to see Carl's face, brushing his hair back from his eyes, feeling his sweat.

"I understand why we have to be quiet, Keith. I do. Believe me. I just hate the injustice to us as a couple."

"We'll live with it." Keith shrugged. "I suppose it gets easier with time."

"It'd better."

"So many other actors are doing it. We have to, Carl. Promise me."

"I will, babe. I promise." Carl kissed him. "Let's shower. I have to get those lines memorized."

Keith climbed off the bed, retrieving the spent condom to dispose of. He felt sick about the lie as well. But that was life.

"You okay?" he asked as Carl reached into the shower.

"Yes. I'm sorry. I don't know what happened to get me so emotional."

"It's the love." Keith smiled. "It chokes me up all the time."

Carl's eyes lit up in delight. He pulled Keith close and hugged him.

Smiling sadly, Keith crushed him in his arms and sighed.

"Yes, hello. Is this the National Inspirer?"

"Yes. What can I do for you?"

"I have some information you may be interested in."

"What kind of information?"

"It's about two male actors who are secretly sleeping together and I think it'll be of significance to you and your readers."

"Which two men?"

"Carl Bronson and Keith O'Leary from Forever Young."

"Do you know this for a fact?"

"Yes. I do."
"Great! Give me the juicy details!"
"I'll be glad to."

Chapter Thirteen

As Keith walked through the studio to their set, he saw Charlotte instructing the camera crew. Four cameras surrounded the bed in Troy Wright's bedroom, including one suspended from the ceiling. "Holy shit." Keith felt his skin crawl.

Charlotte spun around when she heard him. "Hello, sweetie!"

"Is this for our next sex scene?"

"It is!" She approached him and put her arm around his shoulder. "You see," she pointed to the cameras, "this way we can splice together little snippets of the act without actually showing anything x-rated."

"Gulp." Keith meant it as a joke, but seriously felt nervous.

"You'll do fine. Don't you worry about a thing."

She walked back to the crew.

He felt someone lean against him and expected to see Carl. When it wasn't, Keith was very glad he didn't speak his name. "Hey, Cheryl."

"I see it's your turn again."

Keith stood back so he could face her. "Do you and Omar ever get stage fright over the sex scenes?"

"We did slightly in the first season. I suppose we're more used to it now. It must be horrible for two straight men to do it. I feel for you guys."

Carl's crying comments about hiding rang through Keith's mind. "Yes. It's very difficult to fake it with a guy."

"I shouldn't be cocky about it. Charlotte has had two women kiss on one of her past shows. I know my time is coming."

"Will it gross you out?" Keith asked, just seeing Carl coming in behind her.

"I hope not. I just think it'll feel really weird."

"Hi, Keith. Cheryl."

"Hey, Carl. Keith and I were just discussing your next hot sex scene." Cheryl gestured to the set. "Look at all those stupid cameras. You'd think she was doing a colonoscopy the way she has them poised."

"Yipe!" Keith shivered. "Shut up!"

She giggled. "Just kidding. Have fun you two!"

After she walked away, Carl whispered, "Jesus. What's with all the weird camera angles?"

"Charlotte said she gets 'snippets' to splice." Keith shook his head.

"I'm tellin' ya," Carl declared, "It gets Charlotte's rocks off."

"And I'm dying here, Carl. Christ Almighty."

"At least we've had more practice in the bedroom," Carl whispered.

"That's what I'm afraid of," Keith laughed, "We'll get carried away and I'll end up sucking your dick or slipping inside you."

"Wow! That'll go over big."

"Get ready boys!" Charlotte shouted.

"Crap," Keith complained as he walked to the dressing room.

"Let's just try and focus so we do it in one take. I don't really feel like being naked all afternoon in front of the fucking crew." Carl began taking off his shirt.

"I hear ya." Keith greeted their wardrobe man. "Hey, Mel."

"Hello, boys. Ready for yet another x-rated scene?" He held up a robe for each of them.

"No!" they both answered in stereo.

Carl was not getting used to these scenes, nor did he like them. It felt personal now. Like a room full of voyeurs invading Keith and his private life. And being naked on television? It was a nightmare. He was not an exhibitionist, quite the opposite. He knew once these new episodes aired, he'd get so much flack from his friends and family he'd never hear the end of it.

His robe wrapped around him tightly, he and Keith walked barefoot back to the set and the large group behind the scenes who had the pleasure of witnessing it.

As he stood next to Keith he could hear his heavy breathing. He knew Keith's nerves had kicked in as well.

"Okay, boys, listen up," Charlotte began, "Just forget about the cameras and relax."

Carl choked in a laugh.

"All right, Mr. Bronson, I know," she chided. "But I want you two to get swept away this time. Imagine you're really in love and the passion is scorching."

Carl's stomach fluttered. That's easy enough. Just let us be in a room alone!

"Don't worry if it gets awkward, just get back into it. I won't break the action since this is going to be ten second clips spliced into one two minute scene. So all you have to do is enough playing around for a two minute shoot. How hard is that?"

Neither man answered. Carl felt as if she was nuts. How hard is it to roll around naked with another man with four cameras shooting up your ass? Oh, easy-peezy!

"Make it hot. Make it memorable. The preview audience of women is salivating over the two of you. You are the couple making the biggest sensation. I want you to know that everyone is cheering for you to stay together and be a permanent pair."

"I hope so," Keith laughed. "I need the work."

"You're not going anywhere, cutie," Charlotte replied, winking. "Okay. Take a minute to focus and get in character."

Carl put his hand on Keith's shoulder and led him to the stage with the bed. "You ready, Keith?"

"I suppose." Keith released a long exhale.

Carl untied his robe and as it draped open, he closed his eyes and began imagining he was Troy Wright once more. They had very few lines, but were supposed to grunt and moan like they were animals. The lights dimmed and a reddish glow illuminated the bed.

Slowly Carl allowed the robe to drop off and walked past the cameras to the bed waiting for Keith. Forcing his vision to only see Keith, Carl reclined on it, watching him.

After a moment, Keith dropped the robe and joined him. The second Keith did, lying beside him, Carl heard the cameras click on and whir quietly.

Another moment passed before they did anything. Carl touched Keith's face gently. All the dialogue was during their sex act. He closed his eyes and drew Keith into a kiss.

It was so natural, it was almost enough to forget they were being filmed.

He felt Keith shaking slightly from nerves. Wanting to get this over with, Carl decided it was up to him to move them to the level Charlotte craved. And the directions on the script did not indicate quiet passion. She wanted wild heat.

While Keith was connected to his lips, Carl grabbed his shoulders and shoved him back, climbing over him. It seemed to flick the switch inside Keith because he wrapped his legs around Carl's hips. Carl managed to get to his knees with Keith attached to him and thrust against him, hoping something they did resembled fucking. He was still very nervous and his body was not erect.

Keith drew back from their kiss to catch his breath, digging his hands through Carl's hair. Carl began kissing and licking Keith's chest. Keith arched his back, detaching from where he was, dropping down to the mattress with his knees bent and his legs spread wide.

With Keith's fingers massaging his scalp, Carl licked his way downward. As he crossed over Keith's belly button, he realized Keith had a hard-on and if Carl moved any lower he'd have it in his mouth. Trying to think as he went, Carl pressed Keith's legs back, making his cock protrude from his body, and attempted to simulate sucking him. It had to look that way from behind.

When the head of Keith's cock brushed his chin, Carl tried not to panic that someone would notice and judge him.

Faking an orgasm, Keith threw his head back and moaned loudly. The sound made Carl's skin rise with goose bumps and his dick throb.

Once Keith's moans subsided, Carl grabbed his torso and rolled him over. "Get on your knees," Carl hissed silently.

Instantly Keith did, allowing his ass to stick up in the air. No modesty. It was torture.

Carl knelt up, the sweat dripping down his face from his anxiety. He held Keith's hips and rocked against him, his semi-hard cock stroking under Keith's balls.

Dialogue. Dialogue while fornicating.

Carl struggled to remember it. "That's it, baby! You know just how to satisfy your man!"

"Augh!" Keith pretended to be in ecstasy. "Yes! Yes! Harder!"

"No one will tell us we can't be together! No one. You hear me?" Carl slapped Keith's rump. He had no idea why he did it.

"Ah! Yes!"

Now Carl was fully erect. "That's it, babe!"

"Troy! Oh! Troy!"

"Dennis! Dennis! Ah!" Carl thrust his hips forward and made his face a mask of pleasure.

After the pretend climax, Carl dropped down on Keith's back, in turn, Keith fell onto the mattress heavily. Carl wrapped around him, kissing his sweaty neck and cheek. "I love you. I love you, Dennis."

"I love you too, Troy. With all my heart."

Carl didn't know what more they could do. They faked sucking, fucking, and said all their lines. Where was the 'cut!'?

Hissing into Keith's ear, "Shit!" he rolled over and allowed Keith to face him.

Keith pushed Carl's damp hair back from his forehead and kissed him again.

That kiss sent Carl reeling. He wrapped around Keith and sealed him against his body.

Finally he heard, "Cut! Brilliant. Hang on a minute."

Carl sat back from Keith and caught his breath. The woman with the sheet rushed in to shield them. Sitting up, wiping the sweat off his face, Carl waited for the okay. It had to be okay. He didn't want to do this again. It was agony.

"That's fine, boys. Thank you."

Exhaling with relief, Carl reached for his robe as Keith did the same. Wrapping it around him, Carl left the set quickly, feeling queasy to have done that in front of so many people.

Once he was in the wardrobe area, he dropped the robe and slipped on his briefs and jeans.

Keith was right behind him. "Christ! That sucked!"

Agreeing completely Carl shook his head. "I really feel pushed to my limit, Keith."

"Me too. Believe me."

"I feel like we're the new sideshow attraction." Carl looked at Keith as he buttoned his shirt. Keith was zipping his jeans.

"How many scenes like that are we expected to do?" Keith wrestled his T-shirt over his head and tucked it in.

"Who the hell knows?" Carl sat down to put his shoes and socks on.

Melvin interrupted their conversation. "Sex sells, guys."

Trying to calm down, Carl met Melvin's sympathetic gaze. "I realize that, but when does it turn away from sweet romance and into smut?"

"Okay," Mel replied, "I'll rephrase it. Smut sells."

"Please tell me this isn't going to be a regular occurrence," Keith whined.

Melvin shrugged.

After he was dressed, Carl needed to splash his face. He left the room and pushed back the door to the restroom. Leaning over a sink, he rinsed his hands with cool water and washed his burning cheeks and neck. Looking at his reflection he hissed, "You're a fucking porn star, Carl. How do you like it?"

Keith knew Carl was very upset. As he poured himself a soft drink, Keith wondered if it was worse now that they were lovers. It certainly felt like an invasion of their privacy, much more than it did before they were a couple. It was terribly awkward to have their contact filmed.

Sipping his soda, Keith caught a glimpse of Cheryl and Omar's heavy petting. Was this soft porn or was this drama? Keith was beginning to think the lines were being blurred.

Catching movement out of the corner of his eye, Keith found Carl opening a bottle of water to chug. Closing the gap between them, he whispered, "You okay?"

"No. But I'll live."

"She has to keep those scenes limited, Carl. I've watched cable dramas for years and none of them have hot sex scenes weekly."

"Who the fuck knows what she'll do." Carl drank more water.

"Are you going to say something?" Keith became nervous about jeopardizing their roles.

"No. What can I say? I don't want to be written out of the fucking show."

"Exactly. I'm glad you said that."

"But I don't have to like it."

As Carl's lip snarled in distaste, Keith felt like touching him to comfort him. But he knew he couldn't.

"My father will have a coronary when this episode airs."

"Oh?" Carl stepped closer so they could speak quietly.

"Yes. I got into an argument with him over lunch."

"Why didn't you mention it before?"

Keith shrugged.

"About you playing a gay part?"

"Yes. I told him I liked touching you."

Carl choked in shock.

"Shh." Keith gestured that they should move further away from the set.

When they were near the restroom, Carl asked, "What did you do that for?"

"He made some inflammatory remarks about gay men. I felt justified."

"Does he think you're gay now?"

"I don't know, and I don't care."

"Oh? Outted yourself to your parents?"

"Not exactly. I just let him know his homophobia was not appreciated."

"Good for you."

"That doesn't mean I want to come out in public, Carl."

"I know the difference, Keith."

"I placed an ad for a new roommate for Patty."

"And? Where are you going to live?"

"I've been looking in your neighborhood for a studio."

"There aren't many in that area, babe."

"I know."

"You…you want to move in?"

"What?" Keith did. So badly he could cry. "How can we manage that without getting caught?"

"Just because we're roommates…"

Keith cut him off. "Sure, Carl, sure."

"The offer's out there. Your decision."

"Don't do that! I want to! Are you kidding me?" Keith lowered his voice. "I was hoping you would ask me."

"Move in. We can say while we're working together it's economical and better on the environment. Green. Use the word green and carpool and you'll get away with anything these days."

"True. You know, there is some truth in that."

"Who are we kidding?" Carl's eyes sparkled as he smiled.

"Ourselves?" Keith laughed.

"Move in anyway." Carl touched Keith's cheek.

"Yes. What the hell."

"God! I want to kiss you."

"Shh. Let's see how poor Omar and Cheryl are doing."

They walked back to the set to find the other couple had

finished their love scene. Keith knew they had one more scene, dialogue only, to do before they received the new episode and could leave.

Charlotte called Keith over.

"Uh oh." Keith hissed, "What did I do now?"

"Bad boy." Carl laughed.

Putting on a brave smile, Keith approached Charlotte. "Yes?"

"I heard through the grapevine you have a spot on Oprah."

"I do."

"What are you going to tell her if she asks about your personal life?"

"What do you want me to tell her?"

Charlotte laughed heartily. "I want you to tell her you and Carl are real lovers!"

"No. What else do you want me to tell her?"

"At least don't say you're perfectly straight."

"Why not?"

"It'll ruin the mystique. Your fans assume you and Carl are gay."

"Come on, Charlotte." Keith tried to laugh it off.

"I'm telling you, a big part of your popularity relies on appearances. It's like the straight heartthrobs denying they're married so their fans can fantasize they have the potential of dating them. Same thing."

"I will not come out on a talk show. Forget it."

"Then make it ambiguous. Just play the vague card."

Remembering Adam's warning, Keith replied, "I realize the ratings will improve for this show, but I'll be shunned after it ends. I won't do it, Charlotte. I'm sorry."

"Well, the decision is yours. Just don't make it like you're revolted."

"Fair enough."

"You ready for your dialogue with Omar?"

"Yes." Keith looked back at Carl and shook his head at him in frustration. He mouthed, "Talk show appearance."

Carl could imagine that conversation. He'd had the same one before his guest appearance. If Charlotte thought either of them would be her sacrificial lamb, she was mistaken. Hit shows were temporary and fickle. They had to keep their long-term careers in mind.

But at least Keith was moving in. Imaging Keith with him every day, Carl felt his body light on fire. Keith in his bed all night? Every night? It couldn't get better than that. Yes, it was a risk, but they were co-stars, they could claim all sorts of reasons it made economical sense for them to reside together at the moment. After the show ended, they'd see what they would do. Most likely they'd be yesterday's news.

It wasn't that common for men to be outted against their will in Hollywood. The press did keep some sense of propriety. The rags hinted, the gossip alleged, but no one was out and out sent to the stake and burned.

The important thing was that Keith would be with him. That was all that mattered.

Chapter Fourteen

His mobile phone rang just as he was getting out of his car. "Hello?" Keith answered it.

"Yes, I'm calling about the ad in the paper for a roommate?"

"Oh. Great. Yes, it's still available. Do you want to come by and see it?" Keith pocketed his keys and carried his script with him to the lobby.

"Yes. I would. How much is it?"

"It's half the rent, four hundred a month plus utilities."

"Okay. When can I come over?"

"How about now?" Keith checked the mailbox.

"Good. See you in a few minutes."

"Oh, what's your name?" Keith asked before she hung up.

"Karen."

"Okay, Karen." He disconnected the line and climbed the stairs. Good. At least I can move out now without a guilty conscience.

Waiting to eat something for dinner until after Karen had come and gone, Keith paced nervously, reading the script while he did. When the door buzzer sounded, he jumped in response and hurried to react. After pushing the button to unlock the door, Keith opened his front door and kept reading the script while he did.

A young brunette appeared from the stairwell.

"Hi." Keith lowered the script and smiled at her.

"Hey! You're Keith O'Leary!"

He was stunned to be recognized. "I am. Come on in, Karen." Following her inside, Keith tossed the script on the kitchen table.

"I love you in Forever Young. I'm so glad they brought in a gay character."

Keith instantly blushed at the comment. "Yes, well…have a look around. The woman who lives here, Patty, works most weekends and evenings waitressing."

"Struggling actress?" Karen surmised.

"Yes."

"Me too. We'll have a lot in common. Are you leaving because you got the part?"

"I suppose." Keith gestured to the second bedroom. "This will be yours. And it has its own private bathroom as well."

"Are you moving in with Troy? I mean, Carl Bronson?"

His body went cold. "No. Why would I be doing that?"

"Oh. I read in the Inspirer that you two were real lovers."

Imagining the article she was referring to was the one Carl had shown him, which only implicated them, Keith shook his head. Deny, deny, deny.

"No. That's just what people want to think. Both Carl and I are straight."

"Really?" She eyed him suspiciously. "I'm surprised they can get away with that kind of article unless it was true."

"Do you even want to look at the place?" Keith felt like shoving her out. He was not enjoying this semi-public accusation.

"Oh. I want it. I need a place and the price and location are right."

"Great. I'll let Patty know." Keith wanted her to leave.

"When can I move in?"

"Immediately."

"Wow, you and Carl must be hot to trot!"

Grinding his jaw, Keith reiterated, "We are not hot to trot and I am not moving in with him."

"You better check out the paper. They really made it sound serious between you."

"That's publicity, Karen. When you finally get an acting job, you'll understand." He led her to the door.

"I suppose. Don't worry about it though, Keith. Everyone out there supports you two as a couple."

Rubbing his face in frustration, Keith replied, "It's acting. Hello? We act like we're lovers, Karen. There is a difference."

"Sure, Keith. I get it. Okay, I'll start packing and move in as soon as I can. Should I meet Patty first?"

Keith found a pen and paper. "This is her mobile phone number. Give her a call."

"I will. Nice meeting you. Love the show!"

Trying to wave and smile as she left, Keith was so angry he

could punch a wall.

After he got the okay from Patty Keith felt relieved. A day later he and Carl began shifting his things out of the apartment.

Filling a box with his books, Keith didn't own any of the furniture so it wasn't too difficult to get his belongings together. After two trips to Carl's condo, he had pretty much cleared out the apartment of his possessions.

Patty stood by silently as Keith finished filling the last box. "It's really weird that you and Carl are going to be living together."

"Why?"

"I don't know. Don't you think people will get the wrong idea?"

"They already have the wrong idea." Keith folded the flaps in and sealed the carton. "Just ask your new roomie."

"Oh? Does she think the same thing as the rest of the world?" Patty sneered.

"Stop acting like a jerk. You know damn well we're both straight."

"Sure, Keith. Keep that story and stick to it." She laughed sarcastically.

Standing up to confront her, Keith asked, "What the hell's with the attitude? Sour grapes again, Patty? Come on. Lay off."

As they argued, Carl poked his head in the room. "Is that the last box?"

"Yes."

"Great."

Keith stood tall, stretching his aching back. "That's it. I'm out of here now."

"I bet you two can't wait to shack up for real."

"Patty!" Keith caught Carl's anxiety at her accusation.

"Well? You could at least admit it to me, Keith." Patty crossed her arms over her chest.

"Let's go, Carl." Keith nudged him, picking up a suitcase.

Carl lifted the box and headed to the doorway.

"Bye, Carl!" Patty waved, a smirk to her expression. "I'm glad we finally got to meet. Good luck living with your new beau."

"Shut up!" Keith snarled.

"What the hell's your problem?" Carl shouted at her.

"Just go. Ignore her." Keith urged Carl out into the hall.

"Bye bye, boys." She stood in the doorway, waving.

Keith bit his lip to contain his fury and descended the stairs behind Carl.

Once they had loaded the two items into the trunk of the Subaru, Carl climbed into the passenger seat as Keith sat behind the wheel.

"What the hell was that all about?" Carl asked as he belted in.

"I have no idea. I got the same shit from her new roommate, Karen. It sucks." Keith started the car and held Carl's hand.

"What do you mean, from Karen? What the hell did she say?"

"She said she read in the Inspirer that we were going to live together."

"She did? How could they know that?"

"I don't know. Just do what Adam said. Keep denying it."

"Jesus. We haven't even finished moving your things and it's already starting."

"Forget it. I have," Keith lied.

"We need to pick up that newspaper." Carl stared out of the window.

"No. We need to pretend it doesn't exist."

"Yeah, right."

Keith changed the subject. "I'm a sweaty mess. I can't wait to shower."

"Me too. Moving in the summer is painful. Did you tell your parents yet?"

"No." Keith sighed.

"When are you intending on telling them?"

"They have my cell phone number. That's enough."

"Oh, Keith."

"I'm not doing it. I don't need any more grief." Keith tried to relax.

"You have your interview this weekend as well. It's all happening at the same time."

"I know." Keith felt his stomach flip.

"Just keep fucking denying it."

"I will."

"Sucks but it's reality."

"Hey, you don't think I know that? I got that advice from Adam Lewis himself. He knows, believe me."

"He does. Remember that horrible shooting he was involved in? When Jack Turner killed himself?"

"I do. That fucker was vile."

"What's Adam like?"

"He's awesome. Nothing like Turner was."

"I hope not. If he ever asks to suck your cock I'll shoot him!"

"I do have to let Adam know I'm moving."

"Yes. When we get to my place, call him."

"I will. Remind me."

After a shower and a bite to eat, Keith used his mobile phone to call his agent.

"Adam Lewis, can I help you?"

"Adam, it's Keith."

"Hiya, Keith. You excited about your first talk show appearance?"

"Yes. Nervous, actually. But I've moved and I wanted to give you the new address."

"Oh. Hang on…go ahead."

Keith rattled it off. After he did he said, "I'm living with Carl."

"Oh?"

"Yes. Bad idea?"

"Look, Keith, you have to follow your heart."

"I am. I'm just anxious about it. I heard the rags already got wind of it somehow."

"Deny, deny, deny!" Adam laughed.

"Yes. I remembered that advice, believe me. I will." Keith looked back at Carl who was staring at him.

"Okay, Keith. Just be cool and don't worry about it."

"I'll try, Adam. I feel confident we'll be okay. There's no law about being friends."

"No. There isn't. And as long as you stick to your guns about it, you'll be fine. The tabloids don't really violate anyone. They just spout crap and speculate."

"True. That's what Carl has said."

"Well," Adam laughed, "now when Jack and I watch your love scenes it'll have a whole new meaning."

"I know," Keith agreed. "We have to hold back our mouths and cocks." He winked at Carl who chuckled.

G.A. Hauser

"I can imagine. Just don't worry about it, Keith. The two of you are so appealing and talented, you'll be fine."

"Thank you, Adam. I mean that."

"You just call if you need a pep talk."

"I will. See ya." Keith hung up, smiling at Carl. "He makes it seem so easy."

"He's a good man."

Keith approached Carl and knelt on the floor in front of him. "I'm here. Living with you."

"You are."

"Full time."

"Indeed."

Keith opened Carl's shorts. "I need a blowjob rehearsal."

"Blowjob scene! Take one!" Carl revealed his hard-on from his shorts. "Action!"

Keith leaned on Carl's legs and gripped his length, opening his mouth for him. It was just like the script, it became easier with practice.

Sucking him deeply, Keith enjoyed his clean, fresh from the shower taste just as much as his sweat.

"Oh, yes…you really have improved, lover."

"Mm," Keith hummed, lapping at him hungrily.

As Carl moaned in delirium, Keith savored it, knowing he needed to appreciate the things he had in life, for they could be fleeting.

Feeling Carl rise with the pleasure, Keith couldn't wait to taste his come.

"That's it, babe." Carl held onto Keith for balance.

Closing his eyes and sucking to the root, Keith began stroking Carl's balls, feeling them tighten before the climax. Exploring Carl's ass, putting enough pressure on his magic spot, Keith knew Carl was very close.

His fingers tightening their grip on Keith's shoulders, Carl grunted in pleasure and thrust his cock deeper into Keith's mouth. Keith felt his come slide down his throat and moaned in delight, not wanting to stop sucking him.

Drawing on it, milking it with his hand, Keith savored every drop. Finally releasing it from his mouth, Keith looked up at Carl's face. He was recuperating, his eyes closed, his body limp. "Nice."

Carl opened his eyes slowly and let out a soft laugh. "Oh,

God. You are amazing."

When Carl dropped to his knees, Keith wrapped around him, kissing him. "I love you so much."

"Me too, Keith, me too."

The End

Turn the page for a look at

PLAYING DIRTY

Book Two of the Action! Series

G.A. Hauser

Coming in March 2009
Brought to you by Linden Bay Romance

Chapter One

Wearing black jeans, a black shirt, black tie, and back suit jacket, new young cable television heartthrob Keith O'Leary waited backstage at *Oprah* for his introduction. Hearing his name shouted on stage, the AD directed him to go.

Keith felt a mix of excitement and nervousness. His first job acting in a number one hit show had propelled him into the spotlight instantly. The only problem was…he was playing a gay character. And that character just happened to be in love with Carl Bronson, Keith's co-star and secret lover.

What had begun as two straight actors playing a romantic part had morphed into a reality that both Keith and Carl were trying to deal with. Being an out gay actor in Hollywood certainly had its pitfalls. And Keith's agent, Adam Lewis, continuously warned him to be very careful.

With all the internal dialogue spinning through his head from Adam to "deny, deny, deny", Keith felt confident he could keep his private life private, and his professional composure no matter the accusation. He had to. His career depended on it.

He jogged through the curtains to Oprah as they played the theme music for his hit show. Shaking her hand, he waved to the audience and smiled as they cheered wildly.

"Keith O'Leary, ladies and gentlemen! Keith O'Leary!"
Bowing, smiling broadly, Keith couldn't believe the screams from the females in the audience. He was coaxed to have a seat and the noise level finally settled down.

"Well! How does it feel to be the newest rising star on television?"

"Wonderful." Keith smiled as more cheers rang out.

"Obviously, you already have many fans."

"I know! Thank you!" He waved at the audience.

"Your first starring role, your first season, how are you coping with it all?"

"It's overwhelming. But I love it." Keith felt calmer now that he was sitting and talking. The anticipation was worse than the reality.

"Were you hesitant to star as a gay man who is out?"

"No. I enjoy the challenge. I think the show helps to examine alternative lifestyles in a positive way."

Shrieking cheers emerged from the crowd.

"I think many of the ladies are jealous you get to kiss that handsome co-star."

Keith blushed and smiled. "I bet!"

"Is he as nice in person as he seems to be on TV?"

"He's great. Yes. Carl Bronson is a very nice guy."

"Did that fact make it easier for you?"

"Yes. Of course." Keith couldn't wipe the smile from his face.

"Do you get many fan letters from gay men? Thanking you for your support?"

"Not yet. But I assume I will. I'm happy to bring to light a character who can show he's not afraid to love a man. I think too much energy is wasted on ignorance and preventing gay marriage."

"I agree!"

Keith smiled as the audience clapped in support.

"Tell us what else you do. What are your hobbies?"

As Keith talked about his life, he knew things would work out. It all felt right.

Carl wanted to go with Keith and wait backstage but, wisely, he didn't. The last thing either of them wanted to do was verify the already growing suspicion that he and Keith were real lovers. There was no way Carl was ready for that. He wanted a long career on television and especially in films. Unfortunately, out gay men did not get leading roles in romance or action movies. Not to his knowledge anyway.

Reading the new script, waiting for Keith to come home, Carl daydreamed about a time when the men in Hollywood wouldn't have to hide what they did. They weren't there yet. But soon. Maybe soon.

As he heard a key turning the lock of the door, his heart lit on fire. Standing from his position on the couch, he waited for his first glance of the man he adored.

Seeing him come through the door and beaming, Carl knew Keith had done just fine. "Come here, baby."

Keith tossed his keys aside and hugged Carl tight. "I love you."

"I love you too, Keith." Carl crushed him in his embrace and kissed his neck.

"Yes, hello, remember me? I called you last week about the relationship between Carl Bronson and Keith O'Leary."

"Yes. I remember. Do you have anything else we can use?"

"I will soon. How would you like evidence of their relationship?"

"We'd love it. What do you have in mind?"

"A videotape of them together, making love."

"Oh?"

"I just want to know if I went to the trouble of getting it, you would use it."

"Are you kidding? Yes. We'll use it. And we'll pay you very well for it."

"I thought so. Good. I'll be in touch with you soon."

"Great. I'll be waiting."

About the Author:

Award-winning author G. A. Hauser was born in Fair Lawn, New Jersey, USA, and attended university in New York City. She moved to Seattle, Washington, where she worked as a patrol officer with the Seattle Police Department. In early 2000 G.A. moved to Hertfordshire, England, where she began her writing in earnest and published her first book, In the Shadow of Alexander. Now a full-time writer in Ohio, G.A. has written dozens of novels, including several bestsellers of gay fiction. For more information on other books by G.A., visit the author at her official website at:

http://www.authorga.com.

Other works by G.A. Hauser
Available Now!   *Coming Soon:*

A Recommended Read:

Lessons In Love
Charlie Cochrane

St. Bride's College, Cambridge, England, 1905.

When Jonty Stewart takes up a teaching post at the college where he studied, the handsome and outgoing young man acts as a catalyst for change within the archaic institution. He also has a catalytic effect on Orlando Coppersmith.

Orlando is a brilliant, introverted mathematician with very little experience of life outside the college walls. He strikes up an alliance with the outgoing Jonty, and soon finds himself having feelings he's never experienced before. Before long their friendship blossoms into more than either man had hoped and they enter into a clandestine relationship.

Their romance is complicated when a series of murders is discovered within St. Bride's. All of the victims have one thing in common, a penchant for men. While acting as the eyes and ears for the police, a mixture of logic and luck leads them to a confrontation with the murderer—can they survive it?

A Recommended Read:

Secrets and Misdemeanors
G.A. Hauser

When having to hide your love is a crime…

After losing his wife to his best friend and former law partner, David Thornton couldn't imagine finding love again. With his divorce behind him, he wanted only to focus on his job and two children. But then something happened, making David realize that despite believing he had everything he needed, there was someone he desperately wanted—Lyle Wilson.

Young and determined, Lyle arrived in Los Angeles without a penny in his pocket. Before long, however, the sexy construction worker nailed a job remodeling the old office building that held the prestigious Thornton Law Firm. Little did Lyle realize when he gazed upon the handsome and successful David Thornton for the first time that a door would be opened that neither man could close.

Will the two men succumb to the tangled web of societal pressures placed before them, hiding who they are and whom they love? Or will they reveal the truth and set themselves free?

A Recommended Read:

Naked Dragon
G.A. Hauser

Police Officer Dave Harris has just been assigned to one of the worst serial murder cases in Seattle history: The Dragon is hunting young Asian men. In order to solve the crime it's going to take a bit more than good old-fashioned police work. It's going to take handsome FBI Agent Robbie Taylor.

Robbie is an experienced Federal Agent with psychic abilities that allow him to enter the minds of others. You can't hide your secrets and desires from someone that knows your every thought. Some think what Robbie has is a gift, others a skill, but when the mind you have to enter is that of a madman it can also be a curse.

As the corpses pile up and the tension mounts, so does the sexual attraction between the two men. Then a moment of passion leads to a secret affair. Will their love be the distraction that costs them the case and possibly even their lives? Or will the bond forged between them be the key to their survival?

This is a publication of
Linden Bay Romance
WWW.LINDENBAYROMANCE.COM

Printed in the United States
142141LV00005B/10/P